The propeller roared into life, when suddenly—CLANK!—something was wrong.

"Abner! Cut the motor!"

Too late! Smoke poured from Ragwing as the engine ground to a halt.

"What you need now, Abner," said Cornwall, "is a miracle—or a new motor."

Abner stared down at the wreckage. But Cornwall was staring at the Volkswagen parked outside the barn. "Do you see what I see?" he said.

"Right," said Abner, settling back into the cockpit. "Get it. Go get that VW motor . . . !"

THE
SKY'S THE LIMIT

Vic Crume

TEXT ILLUSTRATIONS BY JOSEPH GUARINO

*from the Walt Disney Productions' film based on the
story by Larry Lenville*

PYRAMID BOOKS NEW YORK

THE SKY'S THE LIMIT
A PYRAMID BOOK

Pyramid edition published September 1975

ISBN 0-515-03804-0

Library of Congress Catalog Card Number: 75-15394

Printed in Canada

Pyramid Books are published by Pyramid Communications, Inc. Its trademarks, consisting of the word "Pyramid" and the portrayal of a pyramid, are registered in the United States Patent Office.

Pyramid Communications, Inc., 919 Third Avenue, New York, N.Y. 10022

CHAPTER 1

From their second floor window, Abner Therman III and Billy Norton looked out over the grounds of Wakefield Academy, sparkling and deserted in the morning sunlight.

Billy sighed. "Sure looked different yesterday, didn't it"

His roommate nodded. "Sure did."

Twenty-four hours ago, the driveway circling up to the big front entrance of the school had been bustling with arriving and departing cars and parents who were still stowing away luggage, calling out that it was time to say goodbye. But most of all, the scene had been overflowing with young Wakefielders shouting the usual end-of-term message, "See you in September!"

Billy Norton sighed. "I sure wish we could be *normal* like everybody else. We're the only two guys to have to wait a whole extra day to get called for."

He glanced at his wristwatch. "Say, Three, if your dad's plane was on time you'd think he'd be here by now, wouldn't you?"

Three Therman shook his head. "He'd have to wait for his luggage, and he'd have to rent a car. That takes time. I ought to know—I sure have traveled enough."

"Then how come if you know all those things

we've been standing here looking out the window for about an hour?"

Three grinned and looked back over his shoulder. "Because there's no place to sit down."

There wasn't. Every flat surface, beds, desks, dressers, chairs, were covered by model airplanes. Red, blue, yellow, silver biplanes, monoplanes, props and jets—each little model had its part in showing the history of aviation.

In a place of honor, in front of the chest mirror, was a carefully made World War I biplane. Sunlight gleamed along its delicately wired struts, and a miniature pilot sat in the tiny cockpit. Three looked at it with love and pride. "Boy! Will my dad be surprised. He doesn't even know I've been making models."

A sad look came into Billy's dark eyes. "Wish I had a dad I could show them—" He stopped and looked away quickly. "Maybe," he began again, "when your dad sees all this good stuff, he'll change his mind about your having to spend a whole summer on your grandfather's farm. Gosh! You don't *know* your grandfather. And it's not even a ranch. I thought they'd have ranches, not farms, in California."

Three tried to sound hopeful. "Maybe when Dad sees how interested I am in aviation, he'll probably want to take me around to air shows and stuff like that." He looked thoughtful. "*He* didn't stick around a farm and grow up to be a farmer. He went into advertising."

Billy frowned. "Well, knowing parents, I don't think that means he thinks you can be a pilot right away, or anything like that. But maybe if you came

right out and told him your ideas—. Well, I don't know."

He paused. "Say, Three, if you ever do get to be a pilot, maybe you'll get married and have kids. If you had a boy, would you name it 'Four'?"

Three shook his head. "And have to keep on explaining and explaining about Abner One, Two, and Three? That'd be awful!"

Billy grinned. "I guess that Three is better than if they'd called you Little Abner. But maybe it would be better to have a girl. That way you could name her Abnerella, or something, and your father's feelings wouldn't get hurt."

"What a conversation!" Three exclaimed disgustedly. He turned back to the window. "*Hey!*" he shouted. "He's driving up now! Here he comes!"

Billy rushed to the window and watched a long, shining, blue convertible come gliding to a stop at the front entrance. A tall, dark-haired man stepped out onto the drive.

"Boy, that's some car your dad rented! I bet it gets about one-half a mile a gallon!"

Three wheeled away from the window and started for the door. "Come on, Billy. I want you to meet him. Let's go!" He gave the display of models one last look of inspection. "Boy! Will *he* be surprised! Billy, come *on!*"

"Captain Willoughby's just come out," Billy reported from the window. "He's shaking hands with your dad."

"Billy, let's *go! I'm* the one who wants to shake hands with my dad!"

Billy gave the car in the driveway one last admiring glance. "Okay. Right with you."

Together, the boys raced out into the hallway.

Downstairs, Captain Willoughby, Wakefield's headmaster, and Abner Therman II, walked slowly toward the steps.

"My son's written a lot about you," Three's father said.

"Favorably, I hope," Captain Willoughby smiled.

Mr. Therman looked serious. "I just wish he thought half as much of me. We don't see much of each other, you know. How has he fitted in here?"

"He's done well," the Captain answered. "He's made a lot of friends. Sometimes American youngsters who've been brought up in Europe don't adjust as quickly as he has to life in their own country. He's a fine student, too. You'll want to see his records."

Mr. Therman shook his head. "Oh, I very much want to, but it will have to be another time, I'm afraid. In fact, Captain—ah! Here he is!"

Three, followed by Billy, was starting down the steps at a slow pace quite unlike the rush in the hall upstairs. Both boys looked as dignified as the Wakefield uniforms they wore—sharply creased gray trousers, blue blazers sporting the Wakefield crest on the pocket, carefully knotted school tie in the Wakefield regimental stripe of red and black, and shining black shoes.

Three stretched out his hand. "Good to see you, Sir," he said, trying to keep the excitement out of his voice. But he couldn't keep it out of his eyes, nor out of the grin that spread across his face.

His father beamed and reached out both arms

toward his son. "I'll say it's good to see you, Son."

For an awful second, Three was afraid he was going to be hugged in front of the Captain and Billy. Quickly, he seized his father's hand and said, "This is Billy Norton. He's my roommate."

Mr. Therman quickly dropped his arms, shook hands with Three and then with Billy. "Nice to meet you, Billy," he said. "I suppose—"

Three interrupted. "Come up and see our room, Dad," he said eagerly. "There's something I want to show you. And you're going to be *surprised!*"

Mr. Therman smiled, but shook his head. "I'd like to, but we're on a tight schedule, you know." He turned to Captain Willoughby. "Captain, what's the best way to the airport from here?"

Captain Willoughby glanced swiftly at Three and saw the look of stunned surprise leap into Three's dark eyes. "Sure you can't spare a few minutes, Mr. Therman? We'd all like to show you around Wakefield."

Three's father smiled again. "And I'd love to see it, too. But it's that old tight schedule, you know."

"I understand," the Captain said smoothly. He stepped out along the drive and motioned toward the highway. Three's father followed him.

"Just take a right turn at the gate, Sir," Captain Willoughby said. "You'll be on Arbor then. Keep right on going until you see the access sign for the turnpike. You can't miss it. And the turnpike will take you straight to the airport." He paused. "But I am sorry you don't have time to have a look around here. Maybe in September?"

For a brief second, Three's father looked away

from the Captain. He laughed. "September? That does sound a long time off, doesn't it?" He touched the Captain's elbow, and together they walked a short distance along the drive.

Over by the steps Three and Billy watched the two men talking. Billy looked almost as disappointed as his roommate. "Tight schedule," he muttered. "Just *one* time I'd like to be included in one of those 'tight schedules' they're always on. My mother's schedule is so tight that she couldn't even get here on the day school ended." He shrugged. "But then my mother doesn't care about stuff like model airplanes anyhow, so it doesn't matter much for me. I sure wish your dad could have seen them, though."

Three's shoulders stiffened. "Well, I guess you can see that he's a really high-powered executive. They really *move!*" he replied loyally.

As his father and the Captain turned back toward the car, Three held out his hand to his best friend. "Well—as they say—see you in September."

Billy nodded and shook hands. "Okay. Have fun."

"Fun! Staying three whole months on a crummy farm? No way."

"At least you'll meet your grandfather," Billy replied. "And I guess it's about your only chance if he's so old."

Three looked gloomy. "Old farm, old grandfather. I'll probably come back in September covered with wrinkles, myself."

Billy nodded. He watched Three's father get behind the wheel of the convertible. "Too bad, though, that he couldn't have taken just *one* look.

Oh, well, that's parents for you. So long, Three. See you in September."

Three looked out over the cloud field below the big jet. It was no grayer than his spirits—and no gloomier. None of his arguments had counted with his father, and the plane was almost ready to land. *If* Dad weren't living in hotels instead of a house. *If* Mother were still living. *If* Dad just weren't so busy each day. If, if, if.

Three made one last try. "Grandfather never came to see us," he said. "Why do I have to go see him?"

Mr. Therman put down his magazine. "We were traveling around for years. How could your grandfather come all the way to Europe when I didn't know how long we'd be living in any one place? Be reasonable, Three."

"But I don't want to stay at some crummy farm!" Three burst out.

Mr. Therman slapped the magazine on his knee. "I've asked you not to use that word!" he said sharply.

Three looked back at the cloud field. "It's just a word," he muttered.

His father sighed. "When you've been in the advertising business as long as I have, you'll understand the power of words. Who'd ever buy a book called 'Rebecca of Crummybrook Farm'?"

Three almost wanted to smile. Instead, he remembered that *he* wasn't going to be in the advertising business and his jaw set stubbornly. "Crummy or sunny—I'm not going to like it," he replied grimly. "I'm not the farmer type."

CHAPTER 2

So a disgusted and hurt Abner Therman III sat beside Abner Therman II in the rented Volkswagen heading along the highway to his grandfather's farm.

"We're almost there," his father said. "See that white house over on the left? That's it."

Three looked up ahead. Set far back from the highway was a one-story farmhouse. Not far from it was a slowly turning windmill, and beyond the windmill was a barn. From the highway view, Three could see two small corrals beyond the barn. In one was a single black horse. In the other, were a few steers. On a nearby rolling field stood a tractor. That was it. Ahead, a big clump of trees blocked the view of the driveway. Three's father slowed and made a left turn.

POW! Out from the driveway zoomed a pickup truck. Almost along with the sound of screaming brakes, the front end hood of the little VW popped up.

Three jolted forward then jolted back, his view of things completely cut off by the raised hood. His father angrily twisted the door handle open. "Of all the dumb—" He leaped to the road.

From inside the shadowed VW, Three heard the words, "Dad," "Son!"

And then, "What are you doing in one of those bug cars?"

Three heard his father laugh. "It was what they had for rent at the airport."

"No matter," the other voice cut in. "Not much damage. Nothing Cornwall and I can't fix up in no time. And in case you're in a hurry, you can use the truck. Just leave it with Grimes at the airport and tell him we'll bring this rented bumblebee back to him. Now where's this grandson of mine?"

At those words, Three stiffened back. He straightened his tie and sat erect as though he were on parade drill at Wakefield Academy.

The door flung open. "So there you are! Come on out, Son. Join the party. Come on. Let me have a look at my grandson."

Cooly, Three stepped from the car. He reached out his hand to the tall old man stooping toward him. "Yes, Sir. Pleased to meet you, Sir."

His grandfather pumped Three's hand up and down. "Want to ride back in the truck with me?"

"No. Thank you, Sir."

Grandfather glanced from Abner II to Abner III. Two shrugged. "You lead the way, Dad. Three can stick out his head and guide us in."

"Fine. Cornwall's itchin' to see you."

Three looked away. "Well, I'm not itchin' to see Cornwall—whoever he is," he muttered beneath his breath.

From the time when the VW pulled up to the farmhouse porch, to the time the luggage was set down in the bedroom Three was to have, seemed only seconds.

"This was your dad's room, Son," the grandfather said. "Guess you remember it, don't you, Two?"

Three's father nodded briskly. "Sure do. Well, Dad—sorry I have to run off right away, but I'm on a tight schedule."

"Right *away!*" Three's grandfather stared for a moment, then turning, led the way from the bedroom, back into the farmhouse kitchen. "You know best," he said quietly. "But I thought maybe after this long time we were going to have a real visit —like maybe fifteen minutes."

"It's not that I wouldn't like that, Dad, but—"

"I know," the grandfather said. "You're on a tight schedule."

"That's about it. Well, now—I'll see you both soon."

Three made one last stab at things. "Dad, why can't I go with you?"

"We've been all through that," his father answered sternly. Then he suddenly bent down and gave Three a quick, firm hug. "I'll be back. Do what your grandfather says. Okay?"

Three could hardly believe it was happening. His father was leaving—and leaving alone. "How can he do it when I just about *begged* him to take me?" His eyes stung so hard that he could hardly see as he trailed after his father and grandfather to the porch.

Abner II hopped into the pickup. "I'll leave it with Grimes at the airport, Dad, just as you said. You're sure Cornwall can fix the VW?"

"Sure! Why that Cornwall is a better mechanic than he is a cook!"

Three's father grinned. "If I remember Cornwall's cooking, that isn't saying too much. Say hello to him for me, will you?" And with a cheerful wave, Abner II headed the pickup back down the driveway.

At the highway turn, he signaled a final good-bye with a long blast on the pickup horn. The grandfather's hand went up in a final wave, but not Three's. All of a sudden he felt an almost choking anger. "Now I know," he thought. "With Dad, business comes first."

As his grandfather turned to speak, Three whirled away. Shoulders Wakefield-straight, he marched into the house.

Thoughtfully, Abner Therman looked at the closed kitchen door. "Well now. Looks as though *my* son's just made a big mistake with *his* son. That boy's mad at the world right now, or I miss my guess!"

From the bedroom window, Three saw a man just about as old as Abner Therman come puffing around the corner of the house.

"Where's he goin', Abner?" the newcomer cried out.

"Catching a plane, Cornwall," Three's grandfather replied. "He's got a date with the advertising business."

"In our truck?" Cornwall asked.

"I'll have to explain about that," Abner answered.

Three could hear the disappointment in Cornwall's voice when he spoke again. "He could have said 'hello' or 'goodbye' or somethin'."

"He'll be back," Abner replied. "The boy's inside. Why don't you come in and meet him?"

Cornwall sounded uneasy. "I ain't used to kids around. What do I call him?"

"Three."

"Three! That's stupid. Maybe I should take to callin' you 'One'."

Three heard his grandfather chuckle. "Come on, you decrepit old cowpunch!"

"Old cowpunch? You're an old dirt grubber. How do you like that?"

Three saw the men head for the porch. He took a quick look in the mirror and smoothed his hair. For some reason, he wanted to let both those old men know that he was a *Wakefielder*—not some nobody who dropped his "g's" and probably never had been farther from an old farm than the nearest grocery store.

Abner appeared in the doorway. "Got someone I want you to meet, Cornwall."

Cornwall stepped forward.

Three looked at him cooly. "Are you the hired man?" he asked.

Cornwall's old eyes glinted, and Abner quickly said, "Can we help you unpack, Son?"

"I can manage," Three answered coldly. Then he added, "Thank you. You may take my suitcase later, Cornwall."

Before Cornwall's jaw could drop right to the floor, Abner spoke. "I'll do that, Cornwall. And, by the way, there's one of those bug-size cars in the barn. It's a little banged up. Could you take a look at it?"

Without a word, Cornwall stumped off, and for

a second there was a dead silence in the room. Then Abner asked quietly, "Do you like fishing, Three?"

"I've never fished, Sir," Three replied, making it sound as though fishing was a wonderful thing never to have done.

"Hmm. How about swimming?"

Three perked up. "Oh, you have a pool?"

Abner shook his head. "No. We have a small lake. And a crick, too, when the water's up."

Three stared. "A crick? Oh, I guess you mean *creek*."

Abner's eyes glinted almost as Cornwall's had. But he replied easily, "Maybe so. Tell you what. This is your first day. Why don't you just have a look around? Kinda get your bearings. Okay?"

Without waiting for Three's reply, he turned and left the room.

By the time Three, still in his Wakefield uniform, was ready to go exploring, nobody was in sight. From the barn came the sound of metal on metal. "Cornwall and Abner must be fixing the VW," he thought. "Guess I'll wander around and take a look at that horse."

He strolled along in the direction of the horse corral. A big, old dog sunning himself on a nice patch of cool dirt lazily looked up at him. Three hesitated, then reached down to pet it. The dog barked sharply and added a warning growl. Three jumped back. As he did, a large brown goose loomed out of nowhere. She stretched her wings, honked warningly, and glared at him.

Inside the barn, Cornwall and Abner heard the

barking and honking rise over the sound of Cornwall's hammer.

"What goes on out there, Cornwall?" asked Abner from under the hood.

Cornwall stepped to the window and chuckled. "It's Bo and Mabel. Mabel's got a bead on your grandson. He'd better watch out."

If Three had heard Cornwall, he couldn't have agreed more. Mabel's beady eyes looked ferocious. She waddled closer, neck outstretched and wings spread high. Three backed off.

Nothing could have pleased Mabel more. Three's loser-action seemed to go to her head. Overjoyed, she rushed in close for a strike. Three jumped again, but not fast enough. Mabel's yellow bill nipped at his leg, and the dignified Wakefielder bellowed, *"Owww!* Get away from here, you!"

Mabel, thrilled with the results of her performance, prepared for a second attack. This time Three was quicker. He leaped to one side. Alas! His heel caught and over he went. Mabel hissed in triumph. On orange-webbed feet, she began to waltz around him.

Warily, Three managed to get to his feet and dodge the weaving yellow bill.

From the barn window, Cornwall issued bulletins to Abner. "She's got him on the run," he crowed in delight. Then, as though giving another news bulletin, he added, "I don't carry *nobody's* bags." He looked out the window again. "She's got him on the run for sure. He's goin' hell for leather to the back of the house."

Three, dignity forgotten, panted out of Mabel's rushing pursuit. He circled the house, then made for the front door. Too late. Mabel, like a feathered sentry, was already patrolling the porch. She hissed unpleasantly as he came to a skidding stop at the foot of the steps, then gathered herself for a dive-bomb attack.

Three forgot all about Wakefield Academy and its high standards of behavior. At top speed, he sprinted away and headed for the nearby field.

At the barn window, Cornwall shook his head. "Abner, you got about as much chance of makin' a farmer out of that kid as I have winnin' the National Ro-dee-oh Championship—er, I mean, at my age, of course."

"What's he doing now?" Abner asked.

"Out of sight," Cornwall answered. "He headed up toward the lake."

"Well, if you can't see him, you might as well see this engine," Abner replied. "Come on, Cornwall. Give a look and listen. How does she sound?"

The nearest thing to a happy thought in Three's head was that Billy Norton hadn't been around to see his defeat by a silly goose. Although only the chickens behind the fenced-in chicken run were around to hear, he spoke aloud, "This farm is going to be even worse than I thought."

He trudged along, slapping dust from his blazer and the seat of his pants. The old windmill creaked sadly in the faint breeze and the few steers stared in his direction from the corral. The horse corral was too near dog-and-goose territory, so he decided to head in another direction. He ambled on over a narrow wooden bridge that crossed a muddy wash. "This must be the 'crick'" Three thought.

"Some place for a swim!" He walked on until he reached the rim of a giant pond. "This must be my grandfather's 'small lake.' It's not so bad, but nobody's around to swim with but fish."

Suddenly his attention was caught by the sight of the big caterpillar tractor that he and his father had seen from the highway. It was parked on the far side of the lake.

Three began to walk around the lake's edge, and as he came closer, the big metal treads of the tractor began to look very much like the treads on a military tank. In fact, so much so, that military march music began sounding in his head— sounding so loudly that, by the time he reached the tractor, he was stepping it off as though he were back at Wakefield on parade drill.

He looked up at the tractor seat. "Why not?" he murmured. Immediately, he swung up to the floorboard, and the marching music swelled even louder. For a moment, just like George C. Scott in PATTON, Three stood at attention. Then after a smart salute to the whole empty countryside, he swung his arm full circle in a command to attack.

Leaning forward, he tugged at the big levers and fiddled in an expert sort of way with the controls. It would have been plain to anyone at Wakefield that General Three Therman was about to lead a tank battalion into enemy territory. The band music, heard only in Three's head, rose blaringly. It came to a dreadful crashing halt when the tractor engine suddenly roared into life!

The big earth-mover began to move!

CHAPTER 3

For a second, Three froze in horror. The tractor was pitching forward—straight down the slope to the lake below.

Desperately he fought the steering levers. Useless! The big machine ground down to the water ahead. He twisted every control he could see. Nothing happened. The powerful motor kept on roaring. The huge treads splashed into the lake. Water flung up on either side.

Three closed his eyes. "This is the end! Even if I don't like you, Grandfather, I wouldn't drown your tractor on purpose!"

When he felt water circle his ankles, he opened his eyes. How deep would the lake be? The treads must be churning up the bottom. Water rose higher and higher. "I've heard of captains going down with their ships," Three thought miserably, "but even Patton didn't go down with his tank."

At that moment the tractor took an upward tilt. Water began to stream off its sides and swish from the giant metal treads. Three had one moment of relief—at least the lake was shallow.

But no sooner had the caterpillar treads grabbed dry land, than fresh fingers of fear grabbed Three. He and the tractor were heading straight for the cattle corral! The steers behind the rails sensed the oncoming danger, and their bellows rose above the steady, roaring growl of the tractor. As the treads bit into the corral post as though cutting through matchsticks, the frightened animals stampeded in panic.

Back in the barn, Cornwall and Abner raised their heads.

Cornwall looked puzzled. "Sounds like somethin' spooked those critters," he said. Then he bent toward the VW engine again. "Couldn't be. I must be hearin' things."

"I must be, too," Abner frowned. "Cornwall, cut the motor." He cocked his ear to the sounds from outside.

It took Cornwall no more than a second to not only cut the motor, but to rush to the barn door.

"HOLY COW!" he shouted. "Abner, *look!*"

Abner raced to the doorway. "Cornwall!" he gasped. "Three's headed straight for the wash. He'll never make the bridge! Come ON!"

With Abner in the lead and Cornwall pounding after him, the two old men made a desperate dash to reach Three before disaster struck.

Too late! Abner barely managed to make it over the bridge and leap to the safety of the far bank when the tractor treads clanked down on the planks.

Cornwall wasn't so lucky. He came to a panic-stricken stop right in the middle of the wooden span, and square in the middle of the approaching tractor's aim. "Run!" his brain begged. "Turn and run, Cornwall!" Cornwall obeyed—and tripped. Over he went into the wet, muddy creek bottom just as Three, with only inches to spare on either side of the monster, rolled by.

Slipping, sliding, mud-covered, Cornwall managed to get to his feet. "Abner!" he shouted, as Abner went galloping by on the planking overhead. "Give me a hand up!"

Abner paused only long enough to help his friend scramble up before he rushed after the tractor. Again, too late! It was heading for the chicken run.

Once more Three tried to shove the levers, and once more, it was no use. He pushed with all his strength, and at the last minute squeezed his eyes shut as his "command tank" went barreling into the run.

But scared as he was, he was not as scared as the chickens. Squawking hysterically, they flew in all directions, landing here, there, and on the tractor.

Cornwall and Abner, doing their best to reach the runaway farm machine, were caught in a blinding snowstorm of white chicken feathers. They batted at the birds and batted each other in a vain try to reach Three.

Cornwall was first to fight his way out of the feather blizzard, and he stood frozen at the dreadful sight that met his eyes. Three and the tractor, having gone through one lake, several steers, and a runful of chickens, were now zeroing in on Cornwall's prized possession—his vegetable garden.

It was too much. "My *Victory* garden!" he almost sobbed. "It's almost a goner! I'll be at the mercy of the supermarket!"

Abner came puffing up, blowing feathers from his lips. "Your *garden!*" he exclaimed. "My *windmill!* Look!"

Cornwall saw the danger.

"Come on!" he yelled. "We can catch him. He ain't out of the string beans yet."

Three didn't know if he was riding through string beans or an apple orchard. All he could see was a giant windmill looming ahead. "This is just a dream!" he gasped. "I'm dreaming about my old Erector set!"

SCRRUNNCCH! It was no dream.

Abner and Cornwall arrived only in time to stop the tractor on its mad journey. Abner scrambled up and turned off the motor. Its roar no sooner ended than another roar filled the air. The windmill water pipe snapped. Water gushed like an oil well coming in, catching everyone in the downpour.

Abner's arm went around his grandson. "Cornwall," he bellowed. "Help Three down!"

Cornwall, choking with water and rage, shook his head angrily. "Three!" he yelled. *"Three!* That kid's well-named. He's sure done enough damage for three. They oughta name a hurricane after him!"

He stalked off.

In the farmhouse kitchen, Cornwall, in his long johns, piled wet clothes on the sink drainboard. Abner hadn't yet changed into dry clothes, but Three was in pajamas and bathrobe.

Abner looked at his grandson. "Three," he began.

Three hesitated. Then, tight-lipped, he said, "I was just going to my room, Sir."

"Well, now—don't be too upset about this. It was only an accident."

Only an accident! Three almost burst into tears of rage. "I'd rather get a hundred demerits at Wakefield than have him act so—so *wonderful,*" he thought angrily. "This whole day has been one awful accident, and it started with Dad's 'tight schedule', and then leaving me in this crummy place. I've lost out on a whole summer with him. Now this old farm and two *old* men and until September, too! It isn't *fair!*"

He stared at his grandfather then burst out furiously. "It doesn't matter. I'm leaving in the morning. I didn't want to come here in the first place. My father made me! He'll pay for your old windmill and stuff. I don't like this farm and I don't like—"

Three suddenly stopped. But the unspoken word "you" trembled on the air.

Abner looked at him steadily. And when he spoke, his words were slow. "Three, when your father left you here, he made me responsible. So I'm afraid you'll *have* to stay here until we can talk with him."

Three's angry glance wavered. He knew his grandfather meant every word he said.

"Tomorrow," Abner went on, "we'll go into town and get you some real American clothes. After that, we're all going to pitch in and repair some of the damage around here." He paused. "Okay?"

It wasn't okay at all, and Three wasn't going to say so. Angrily he walked out of the kitchen.

In the silence that followed, Cornwall eyed his old friend. Abner's broad shoulders were slumped the least bit, and by the downward tilt of his head, Cornwall knew how much Three's words had hurt. Abner had waited a long time for this visit, and now everything was turning out wrong.

Cornwall swallowed. "What that kid needs is a good seat warmin'. If I was you, Abner, I'd *let* him leave."

Slowly, Abner shook his head. "No, Cornwall. The way I see it, being a grandfather is about the last important thing a man has to do in his lifetime. That boy's my grandson." He looked down, then lifted his head. "We'll work it out. We'll have to."

Three hadn't expected much of a town, but he had thought that the main street might be more than just a block and a half of little stores and one medium-size supermarket.

Abner swung the VW up to the curb and parked in front of the town's one and only police car—a spic-and-span white model with black trim.

"Here's where we get out, Three. We're going over to Gertie's Dry Goods Store, across the street."

Without speaking, Three stepped from the car and Abner strode around beside him.

"Say, Abner," a voice called out. "You can't park there." The town's Chief of Police came hurrying up, a green-tipped paintbrush in hand.

Abner looked back at the VW. "Been parking

there all my life, Chief. You figure on putting in a fire hydrant?"

The Chief pointed angrily at the fresh green paint curb markings. "It's my new loading zone and you've ruined it already! Look at those footprints!"

Abner scratched his head, "Got to give you credit, Chief. Every time you go to San Francisco, you come back with some of these new scientific police ideas. Makes a body feel mighty secure, I'll say that."

As he and Three stepped back they immediately made bright green tracks on the walk. Steaming mad, the Chief yanked out his ticket book, then slapped down his wet paintbrush on the gleaming white hood of the prowl car. Hastily, Abner took the written-out ticket and hurried off with Three before the Chief could notice the prowl car hood and blast off for the moon.

Never in his life had Three been in a store where the owner was summoned by a shout. But Abner yelled out, "Gertie! Where are you?"

What seemed to be a tall stack of brightly colored bolts of cloth walking on legs came down the aisle toward them. Miss Gertie Spencer swung them to the counter, peered through her glasses at Abner and Three, patted her hearing aid, and said crisply, "There is no need to yell, Abner. I can still hear, you know."

"Land sakes, Abner," she continued, "I never saw you here in the morning before. Why aren't you working? And who's this with you?"

Abner put his hand on Three's shoulder. "Want

you to meet my grandson, Abner Therman III. You can call him Three."

Miss Gertie smiled. "Happy to meet you. Knew your father. Everybody called him Two, so I guess it's reasonable to call you Three."

She didn't wait for Three to even say "How do you do," but turned right back to Abner.

"Abner, I haven't seen you for ages. You're looking a little seedy. It must be that Cornwall's cooking."

"Now, Gertie—stop picking on Cornwall and take us down to the boys' section. I need some American duds for my grandson, here. You know —plaid shirts, Levis, and so on. And he needs a good hat. Got any Stetsons on hand? Cowboy type, you know. I've always said that a man's hat should reflect his character."

Gertie took off her glasses and polished them on a corner of her yard goods. Putting them back on her nose, she stared at Three. "He looks just fine to me in the duds he's wearing. Like he stepped out of a magazine or something. Why do you want to dress him like a scarecrow?"

Instantly, Three decided that there was one person in California he liked.

Abner went striding down the aisle, leaving Three and Miss Gertie to follow. And when they finally left her store, Three had plaid shirts, Levis, boots, and the Stetson hat.

"Like 'em, Three?" Abner asked.

Three shrugged. "Okay, I guess. I certainly want to save my Wakefield clothes for Wakefield." He looked squarely at Abner. "Wakefield's pretty American, Sir—even if it isn't a farm."

Cornwall was astride his black horse rounding up steers when Abner and Three returned.

"I'll get on over to the corral and work on the wiring while you get into your work duds. Cornwall's going to need plenty of help with the fence posts after he rounds up those steers," Abner said.

To Three's surprise, the red plaid shirt, blue Levis and soft boots looked and felt pretty good. He reached for the Stetson hat. "This is silly. It's not as though I'm going to be riding the range or anything. But I guess I'd better show up wearing it."

He looked in the mirror and tried out a left tilt, a right tilt, forward, and pushed back. No matter how it sat on his head, he had to admit it looked great. He gave the broad, roll-up side brim a sharp pat. "Well, here goes a real cowhand—ready to round up chickens, I suppose."

There was more to rounding up even one chicken than Three had imagined. Chase, dive, miss. Chase, dive, grab. By the time Cornwall was ready for help with the fence posts, Three's new clothes looked just about like Cornwall's and Abner's old outfits.

"Now your job is to hold the post steady, while I take a swing at it," Cornwall informed him sternly. "Got it?"

Three nodded and bent down for a firm grip on the post. Every time Cornwall's heavy sledge came pounding down, Three expected it to land on his new hat. But Cornwall was right on target every time. "Anyhow," Three muttered, "this isn't much worse than getting those steers back in. At least I won't get knocked down by the corral gate while the thundering herd thunders by. What a life!"

It certainly took longer to get the farm back into some sort of shape than it had taken Three to knock it apart. By the time the windmill, with the help of the tractor, had been repaired and set back in place, Three was so tired he could hardly stick one boot out in front of the other. "If that Cornwall says I have to help get supper, I'm quitting," he muttered. "I'll just tell him I didn't drive the tractor through his old kitchen."

But Cornwall didn't ask. In fact, when he caught Abner standing by the steaming stew kettle, his temper flared. "Abner, don't you start seasonin' my stew."

"I wasn't," Abner replied. "What's wrong with you, Cornwall? I was just tasting it. Been tasting it for years, haven't I?"

Cornwall took the long wooden spoon Abner held and pushed him away from the stove. "Where's the dude?" he asked.

"In his room."

Cornwall chuckled. "Sacked out asleep, I bet. Like I told you, Abner—that kid will never make a farmer."

"You can't say he didn't work pretty hard today," Abner said.

Cornwall grinned. "A little sweat won't hurt him none. Say, cut the bread, will you? We'd better get supper over and drive the bug car back to the airport. We need the truck."

Abner yawned. "We'll let that job go until morning. We can get up early." He thought a moment.

"But we'll let the boy sleep in. No use getting into this farm life too fast."

"Might discourage him, you think?" Cornwall chuckled.

Abner grinned. "Might."

CHAPTER 4

When Three woke up there were no cheerful breakfast sounds or scents coming from the kitchen. He looked at the clock. "Gosh! No wonder. Nine-fifteen."

He pushed back the covers and swung his feet to the floor. "They're probably already out there still fixing up stuff I smashed, and that Cornwall's saying 'that kid's as stupid as his name.' Well, might as well get into those 'American' clothes and be stupid some more."

It wasn't until he reached the barn, still munching his favorite breakfast of a peanut butter and jelly sandwich, that he realized he was alone on the farm. The VW was gone.

Three ambled around the barn. He didn't see anything of great interest until his glance went up toward the level of the hayloft. *Twang!* Three could feel himself thrum like a guitar!

Overhead, hanging from the topmost rafter, was a big, dust-coated, life-sized *1920's biplane*. "Why, it's my plane!" he gasped. "It's a full-scale model! No! It's *real!*"

He stared upward. Though the fuselage covering hung in tatters, and even from ground-level Three could see that the tires were soft and rotted, the skeleton outline was all there, even to the con-

necting metal struts that joined the upper and lower wings at either side.

"I've got to get a closer look," he muttered excitedly. "It's hung up there somehow. How did anybody get it up?"

His glance went around the barn. In less than seconds he spotted the rope pulley that held the plane high above him.

He circled around, still staring upward. Faint, but still visible, he could see the letters painted alongside the plane's nose—RAGWING.

"*Ragwing*. Sure looks ragged! But I bet I could lower it down. Just *easy*, so it wouldn't crash."

The first problem was the tie-off knot on the rope pulley. It was out of reach. Three dragged a heavy crate over and stepped up. The knot was in easy reach of his fingers. As he worked at it, the rope loosened a little bit. Ragwing shuddered, and a sunlit cloud of dust began drifting downward.

Three anxiously braced himself to withstand the down drag of Ragwing's weight on the rope. He gave the rope another careful loosening twist.

At that very same moment, Mabel, the goose, true to her loyal feelings about guarding the Therman farm, wandered into the barn. Instantly, she hissed a challenge to her personal enemy. And at the same time, she snaked out her long neck to zero in on Three's ankles.

Between the ragged bird above and the brown bird below, Three lost his balance on the crate.

There was a loud whine. The pulley rope gave way! Ragwing, like a shot duck, plummeted to the barn floor. Mabel shrieked in alarm. This must have been the biggest bird one brown goose had ever seen. In the cloud of dust that folded over the biplane, she fled, honking wildly, and leaving Three sneezing and alone with this wonder from the barn heights!

As the dust cleared, he hurried to examine his find. With some of the dirt shaken off, it looked in better shape than he'd thought it would be. Even with tires beyond hope and rotted rips in the fuselage skin covering, the wing struts were at least still in place, and its skeleton looked okay.

Three stepped up to the engine cowling. "It's real, all right," he breathed. "If only Billy Norton could see this!"

Almost as though he thought that Ragwing might suddenly disappear before his eyes, he reached out and gently touched the tattered sides. "It's real, all right," he breathed.

Then slowly he inspected it—from tail rudder to the old propeller and engine cowling. "The skeleton looks okay," he muttered. "Needs new struts. New tires. But the prop isn't split, or anything, and there's a *real* engine."

Three went into action. Scrambling up through the grimy dust, he got into the cockpit. The old leather seat belt was cracked and dry, but at least it was there. And just like his own model plane, there was the joy stick—the old-fashioned steering device many a World War I ace had used to climb and dive in the skies over France. Three pushed it forward, back, and from side to side. He tried out the foot pedals. "Bank to left," he murmured. "Bank to right." He pulled back on the joy stick. "Climb!" Already he felt that he was heading for blue sky. In fact, he was so high in the clouds that he didn't hear the farm truck come up the drive.

But he crashed back to earth when Cornwall's horror-struck voice yelled at the barn door. "Holy smoke, Abner! It fell on him! I told you we should've gotten rid of that wreck!"

As the two old men raced into the barn, Three popped up guiltily from the cockpit.

Cornwall skidded to a stop. "That figures!" he exclaimed in disgust. "*Me* worryin' and *him*—I should've known better!"

Abner hurried up by the cockpit. "You all right, Son?"

Three couldn't believe his ears. "No lecture— and after what I did with his tractor!"

He flushed. "I'm sorry I let it down, Sir. It was an accident. I—I just wanted to look at it."

Abner held out his hand. "Sure. Sure. You'd better get out, though. You're getting pretty dirty."

Three took a quick glance at his grimy clothes. "They sure are beginning to look lived in, I guess."

"That's what duds are for around here," Abner grinned, helping Three down to the barn floor.

Cornwall eyed the plane then looked up at the rafters. "Abner, I haven't worn my good hat in here for years. Afraid that contraption would fall on my head. While we got her down, why don't we haul her to the dump?"

"The *dump!*" Three almost shouted. "You can't do that. Why, it's a classic."

"Not 'it,'—'she'," Abner said almost absent-mindedly. He, too, was staring at Ragwing.

"Okay—she," Three replied quickly. "But you

can't send *her* to the dump. I bet there isn't another plane like her in the whole country—maybe the whole world. She's a classic."

Cornwall marched for the barn door. "Classic!" he flung back over his shoulder. "She's a classic if that means you've just found a new word for *junk*."

Three looked up at Abner. "He's all wrong about that, Sir. Lots of people collect old planes. De Havilands, Jennies—all kinds."

Abner eyed Three curiously. "Where'd you learn all that?"

"I build them," Three answered promptly. "That is—I mean models. Billy Norton, he's my best friend—we build them. Our room at Wakefield is full of them."

Abner looked interested, and it seemed to Three that he saw a look of respect come into his grandfather's eyes. "Is that so!" Abner paused. "I built Ragwing myself. She was the first private plane around these parts."

If Abner had been watching Three, he would have seen a look of respect leap into his grandson's eyes. But Abner had turned to Ragwing and was slowly rubbing grime away from the faded letters.

"Ragwing!" he said softly. "What a sweetheart she was, this little plane. Like a bird, she used to seem to me. I remember even the kit I bought to build her. And I used a Henderson motorcycle motor. Four cylinder."

Three watched him. "You're not going to let him take her to the dump, are you?"

Abner sighed. "No, of course not. We'll just haul her back up out of harm's way."

Three hesitated. "Did you ever think of fixing it—her—up?" he asked hopefully.

Abner shook his head. "Oh, years ago—yes. But I'm afraid it's kind of late now to think about that."

"It—it wouldn't take too much, Sir," Three urged. "All she needs is cleaning up and—and new tires. Maybe some—" He broke off and looked almost shyly at his grandfather. "I'd help."

Abner looked thoughtful. "I don't know, Three. Pretty tall order for just the two of us."

"We could do it, Sir. I bet even Cornwall would help."

Abner burst out laughing. "Cornwall help? I'd be afraid to ask him. I can just see his face now!"

But Abner did ask, and the very next day, right after lunch as he and Cornwall were doing the dishes.

Cornwall's eyebrows went up, and his jaw went down. "Abner!" he exploded. "You're gettin' *see-nile.* Do you know that?" He shook his head. "And in case you don't know that word, it means you're gettin' old and silly-actin'."

Abner grinned. "Old, all right, though it seems looking back on the last few days we've both done a heap of racing around for two old men. But silly? Not yet. I figure that a few repairs here and there, and Ragwing would be as good as new."

Cornwall's eyes narrowed. "You didn't promise to take that boy up, did you?"

Abner looked down at the plate he was drying. "I didn't say anything about it. I just said I'd think about it."

Cornwall shook his head. "I done a lot for you, Abner, but I gotta draw the line someplace. And this is where. Besides, his dad'd croak!"

Abner grinned. "What he doesn't know won't hurt him—or Three either. That boy needs—" He held up his hand. "Ssh. Here he comes."

Three, in clean clothes, rushed into the kitchen. "Are we going to do it, Sir?" he asked eagerly.

Cornwall stared unpleasantly. "Do what, may I ask?"

Abner wigwagged behind Cornwall's shoulder and shook his head. "Why don't you run along outside, Three. I'll catch up with you as soon as I've finished up with the dishes."

Three looked sharply from his grandfather to Cornwall, then without a word, walked out of the kitchen. But his heart was making happy thumps. "I *think* Abner's on my side!"

And for the first time since he had left Wakefield Academy, Three Therman wasn't longing for September to arrive!

He hurried along toward the barn, his thoughts all on a bird named Ragwing, not on a bird named Mabel.

He failed to see her beady-eyed head come peering around the corner of the porch. This hissing and honking missile was halfway to her target before her would-be victim could even begin a wild sprint for the shelter of the barn.

But Mabel was in no mood for anything short

of complete victory. She came bolting up after him, firing away her finest honks and hisses.

Three made it into the barn and rushed for safety behind Ragwing. Mabel was not to be stopped. She closed in for the attack, and her yellow bill caught him so hard on the ankle bone that he could feel it through his leather boot.

He danced in pain and rage. "I've had enough of you!" he yelled angrily. And with one sweep of his Stetson, he swiftly plunked it over Mabel's outraged head.

She must have been shocked beyond belief, as part of her feathered frame kept going east while the rest of her tumbled in a northerly direction. She rolled over, honking up a storm, and orange feet slapping the air. Hardly was she once more upright, than Three came swinging in again. "Get out of here, you stupid goose!" he shouted, chasing her to the barn door. "Out!"

Once more Mabel saw the big hat coming her way. Shocked beyond more than one last desperate *honk,* she fled. And dignity lost, she waddled and wobbled as fast as she could go, heading for the corner of the house.

"And don't come back!" Three yelled after her. He gazed for a moment at his Stetson, blew a feather off the brim, then placed the hat back on his head.

From the kitchen window, Abner and Cornwall viewed the outcome of the battle with delight.

"See the way he blew that Stetson?" Cornwall crowed. "Looked like he was coolin' a smokin' six-shooter!"

"Tell *me* we can't make a farmer out of that boy!" Abner exclaimed.

Cornwall's face changed. "Not with no airplane, you can't."

"Don't be too sure," Abner said stubbornly. "Take my word for it. Ragwing's the answer."

Cornwall looked serious. "Abner, fixin' up that old wreck's just too much work. And you take my word for *that*. Besides, the boy's here on the farm. You didn't expect him to stay forever, did you? Why, anyone could tell a mile off that there's only one thing that kid cares about—and that's that Wakefield place. Can't wait to get back to it."

Abner hesitated. "I guess that's it, Cornwall. I want something more for him to love besides a school. It seems as though all his dad has to love is a job. I don't want Three growing up just loving a place or a thing. And I aim to see that they *both* get something more out of life." He cleared his throat. "Love, I mean. That's what I want them to have."

Cornwall turned as red as a poppy. Much to his relief, Abner, too, seemed to feel silly talking about love, because he let a coffee cup slip from the drying towel.

"My china! Abner, you've busted one of my best cups. It was hand-painted, too!"

He bent down and silently tried to fit the two largest pieces together. It was a full minute before he finally looked up at his old friend.

"Well, Abner—you know I'm not for no fixin' up Ragwing. But—" he hesitated. "Okay. Why don't you and the kid get the stuff you'll need from town. I'll—I'll give it a whirl."

CHAPTER 5

Three walked over to Abner's truck where it was parked in front of Gertie's Dry Goods Store. It was already well-loaded with plywood, wire brushes, steel wool, steel cable, and airplane dope. Three added a sack of paintbrushes then walked on into the store.

Miss Gertie was counting out change into Abner's hand. "There. That makes twenty," she said. Then she leaned her elbows on top of the large package that rested on the counter. "Now, Abner, I never learned anything by just minding my own business," she said, her eyes snapping and twinkling behind her glasses. She patted the bundle on the counter. "Why won't you tell me what you're going to use this fine Irish linen for?"

"Patching," Abner answered, smiling. He looked down at the piece of paper he held in his hand.

"Patching what?" asked Gertie.

"Just patching," Abner grinned broadly.

Gertie suddenly plucked the sheet of paper from Abner's hand. She studied the rough drawing on it. "Abner Therman! You're *not*. You wouldn't!"

"I already am," Abner replied calmly.

Gertie gasped. She looked at Three and then at Abner. "Abner, I've known you about as long as forever, and I've known you to do silly things. But *this*." She tapped the sheet of paper furiously. "An airplane! If there's one thing that will kill you faster than Cornwall's cooking, it's flying around in that Ragweed of Earwig—or whatever you call it."

Hurriedly, Three reached for the big package. "Guess we ought to be going, shouldn't we?" he asked uneasily, eyeing Miss Gertie's outraged face.

Miss Gertie didn't even look at him. She leaned forward over the counter. "Abner Therman— you're *not* going to be that silly, are you?"

Abner hastily took the package from Three's arms. "Better let me carry that, Son. Weighs a ton." He tipped his hat to Miss Gertie. "Be in soon again, Gertie. See you later. Goodbye."

Cornwall, watching from the barn door, saw Abner leap spryly out of the truck. "Heck! He got down out of there just about as easy as Three," he thought. "Maybe havin' that kid around is makin' him younger." He rubbed his chin. "Maybe it's hapenin' to me, too. Danged if I don't feel pretty spry myself. Guess it was time for a change around here for us two old duffers."

Three strode up to the barn, carrying as much as he could in one trip. "How long do you think it'll take to fix her up?" he asked Cornwall eagerly.

"Oh—not too long if we work at it."

Abner walked up with the plywood. Three turned to him. "If we put up some lights out here, we could work at night."

"Could be," his grandfather replied. "Let me think about that." He put down the plywood. "Come on. We've lots more to unload."

"Yes, Sir." Three started for the truck and Abner followed.

"Hold on a minute, Son," he said, as Three reached up for a big carton. "Don't you think this 'sir' stuff has kind of run its course? We're kin, you and I. And besides, two fellow airplane builders can't be that formal."

Three hesitated. "Well—"

"The name's Abner—if 'Grandpa' sticks in your craw," his grandfather said.

Three looked down, up, then grinned. "Okay— Abner," he replied.

Late afternoon the next day, Three, rag in hand, stepped back to admire the progress they had made. "Boy, I wish Billy Norton was here to see this. This is going to be the biggest *model* plane in the whole world."

"Who's Billy Norton?" Cornwall asked as he scrubbed along Ragwing's tail section.

"My best friend at school."

Cornwall scrubbed on. "You're really nuts about that school, ain't you?"

Three nodded. "Sure. It's really great. I can't wait to get back in September." He paused. "When I tell 'em I flew in a real biplane—well, it'll blow their minds."

Cornwall's hand stopped mid-scrub. "Going UP!"

Abner's head suddenly appeared above the opposite side of the tail section.

Cornwall marched around the little plane. "Who said anything about him goin' up?" he asked sternly.

Three raced around to join them. "You *are* going to take me flying, aren't you, Abner?"

Cornwall almost brushed Three off his feet. "I ain't about to build one of them Kamikaze planes, Abner. I've been restorin' Ragwing. Now how about it?"

"Just hold on. Both of you," Abner replied. He looked at Three. "I'm only thinking about it. And I won't get it all thought out until I know she's safe. It's not that I wouldn't take you up, but I don't want you to be disappointed if it doesn't work out."

"Then we'll be going," Three said cheerfully. "We know we can get her to fly—fly safe, I mean. I was just telling Cornwall about getting back to school and telling all the guys about really flying. All they've seen me do is make models."

Abner looked at Cornwall's stern, disapproving face, then back to Three. "Tell you what, Three. You've put in a good day's work. Let's knock off. Take a walk. I've a favorite spot around here I'd like to show you."

Three wondered why Abner thought that the top of a long grassy hill was worth the uphill climb. "Nothing but plain old fields to look at," he thought as he flopped, panting, to the grass.

His grandfather stretched down beside him, and together they stared up at the gold and blue bowl of sky. Bo, who had followed along, chased imaginary rabbits.

Three reached for a blade of grass to chew on. "Was Ragwing the first plane you ever flew?"

Abner propped himself up on one elbow. "Ragwing? Nope. Not Ragwing. It was back in World War I. Flew a Spad then."

Three sat bolt upright. "A *Spad!*" he exclaimed. "You mean you were a fighter pilot?"

"Sure was," Abner nodded. "Spads—they were French-built planes." He thought a moment. "I remember when I fought Baron von Richthofen."

"You fought the Red Baron?"

Abner chuckled. "Sure did. Only he put a hole right through my tail feathers."

Three's eyes widened. "Did you crash?"

"Not that time. His guns jammed. Or maybe he ran out of bullets. Who knows? Anyway, we flew along side by side for a while, figuring out what to do with each other. There we were—glaring back and forth. Then I don't know just how it started, but we both began laughing. Laughed so hard, we almost flew into each other. He waved once, smiled, and flew off. That's about all I remember—his smile."

Three was almost reliving that sky adventure. "Did you ever see him again?" he asked.

"No. Never did." Abner was silent a moment. "He was killed two days later."

"That was a long time ago, I guess," Three said, almost sadly.

High overhead, a jet tracked across the blue sky. Abner shook his head. "Now look at that. Jets! Progress! And you can't even see the land from one of those things."

"But clouds are nice, too," Three replied. "They're sort of mysterious."

Abner waved his arm toward the gold and green fields. "Well, I say it's a blessing we've still got the land."

Three looked off into the distance. "Is all this yours, Abner?"

"Not all. But much as a man can use." He patted the ground, then scooped up a handful of earth. With the tip of his finger, he tasted a bit of it.

Three stared.

"Won't that make you sick?"

"Nope. A good farmer can tell the condition of his land by the taste of it. Try some?"

"No thank you," Three answered politely, then added, "I don't believe I want to become a farmer, so I guess there's no use in tasting land."

Abner poured the scooped-up soil from hand to hand. "Here, Three. Hold out your hands. Feel it."

"Why, it's warm!" Three exclaimed. "That's funny."

"Sure it's warm. It's a living thing—like plants and trees and flowers and grain."

He flung himself back on the grassy carpeting. "Know what I think I'll do? Roll down this old hill. Bet I can beat you to the bottom!"

And to Three's amazement, his creaky grandfather began gently rolling over and over down the slope.

"Don't worry about your clothes," Abner called back. "Wash 'n' wear. You'll have to give yourself a fast push to catch up with me."

Three pushed off. Old Bo came over to join the fun, leaping excitedly back and forth between

them. They went faster and faster, until all three wound up in a somersaulting heap on level ground. Abner began laughing until tears came into his eyes. He pulled out a handkerchief and dabbed at them.

"You're all right, Abner, aren't you?" Three asked anxiously.

"All right?" Abner chuckled. "Say, I'm so all right that I can't believe it. We should have had Cornwall in on this. He could stand some limbering up, too!"

Three giggled. "It would sure give him the feel of the land in a hurry, wouldn't it?"

Three turned in early after supper. There wasn't much to do in the evenings around the farm but listen to the radio. Besides, tomorrow he wanted to get in a lot more work on Ragwing.

"Abner talked a lot about land and how you get to love it," he thought sleepily as he lay in bed. "But I wonder how anybody who fought the Red Baron could just—well, just go around loving *land*. I love the sky, myself."

At that point, Abner came into the bedroom. Three sat up. "Hi."

Abner smiled. "Bet you were just going to turn off that radio. You look mighty sleepy to me."

"Oh, I was just thinking," Three replied.

"Oh? What about?"

Suddenly, Three didn't want to tell Abner. He thought quickly. "I was just wondering—how come you don't have a television set, Abner?"

"Tried it once," Abner replied. "No good. We don't get any sound hereabouts. And the picture is tweedy-looking. No point in having one." He turned to the door. "Well, guess I'll go back to the kitchen and read the mail. Haven't had a chance to get at it. Goodnight, Son."

"Goodnight, Abner. Say—" Three pushed at his pillow.

"Yes. Say what?"

Three grinned. "Oh, I was just going to say— I'm glad the Red Baron didn't get you."

Abner smiled. "So am I, Three. So am I."

Cornwall was hidden behind the daily newspaper when Abner walked into the kitchen to shuffle through the small stack of mail on the table. One letter caught his attention. "Now why would Wakefield Academy be sending me a letter? Maybe school's opening a week early or late, or something." He slit open the envelope.

"Holy smoke!" he exploded.

Cornwall lowered the newspaper. "What's wrong?"

"I opened a letter to Three by mistake."

Cornwall lifted the paper again, "Well, that's not the end of the world, is it?"

Abner shook his head. "It will be for him. That idiot son of mine! He's gone ahead and taken Three out of that school without even telling him first." He stood up. "And you got to be deaf, dumb and blind not to know what that Academy means to the boy!"

Cornwall looked nearly as shocked as Abner. "You sure would!"

Abner strode to the telephone. "I'm phoning Two and telling him he'd better get down here right away if he doesn't want a broken-hearted boy on his hands. *I'm* not going to be the one to tell Three, and he isn't going to get the news from the school before he gets it from his dad, either!"

Cornwall listened to Abner's side of the conversation. "You know that Three's going to be fit to be tied when he hears about this, don't you? That school's country, home and mother to him right now. You'd better get down here."

There was crackling on the other end of the line, then Abner said in a calm voice, "Sure. Sure. I know. Do your best. I'll see that the boy doesn't hear about it until you get here."

When Abner put down the phone, Cornwall spoke up from behind his newspaper. "Heard your side. What's Two's side?"

Abner shoved his hands in his pockets. "Two figured a school in San Francisco would be handier. Handier for *him*. He's going to be working on the West Coast now, and this way he could see Three now and then." He sighed. "That's about it."

Cornwall looked around the corner of his paper. "And what did he say about gettin' himself down here?"

"Can't get away right now," Abner said, shortly. "Business, I guess. But he said he'd come as soon as he could, even if it's just for overnight."

"Overnight!" Cornwall exclaimed. "That must be some important job he has." Cornwall shook his head. "No wonder that kid loves his school. Looks to me like it's been his best bet. At least it's *there*— and that's more than his dad is."

Abner sighed again. "I guess Two is trying to do his best."

"Some best," Cornwall growled. "Good thing you did open that letter, Abner. At least the kid can enjoy life until his Dad breaks the glad news. *Hhmphh!*"

CHAPTER 6

To Three, Ragwing already looked like a new plane. Even in the bright morning light that flooded into the barn, her dusty, hopeless look was gone. He gazed at her with pride.

"We've still got a way to go," Cornwall said. "I've got to get to work on the motor. Three, how about you takin' that brush and steel wool and startin' in on the cockpit?"

"Okay," Three scrambled up and over. "Hey, Abner," he called out. "What's this thing behind the seat?"

Abner, working on the wings, glanced up. "Oh, that's for crop-dusting." He edged over to the cockpit. "See that lever? You pull up here and the dust —insecticide, that is—comes down there."

He scooped a handful of yellow dust. "By golly! Still got a supply."

Three's eyes shone. "Suppose we could dust something?"

Abner chuckled. "Well now, Three, I haven't done any of that since—'sakes!—I don't know when. I'm a mite out of practice."

"But just once?" Three begged. "So's I could tell the kids at Wakefield I did it?"

Abner began to climb down. "We'll see what we can do," he said gruffly.

At the plane's nose, Cornwall called over. "Abner, come here a minute. Got a problem."

Three followed after his grandfather, anxious to know what was wrong. Cornwall was waving a wrench toward the motor. "It's pretty old, Abner, and it's been sittin' out here in the barn a pretty long time. I'm worried some of the metal just wouldn't hold up."

Abner shrugged. "Could be. Only way to find out is to give her a good test."

Before Cornwall could argue, Abner turned away. "By the way, Cornwall," he called over his shoulder, "I forgot to tell you the other day—Gertie sends you her love."

Cornwall's voice changed from worried to grumpy. "I don't want it," he called back loudly.

"What do you mean, you don't want it?" Abner chuckled. "That girl has a heart of gold—and she's a good cook, too."

"Good cook!" Cornwall shouted. "Well, if there's one thing I don't need it's a good cook."

But Three stared from Cornwall to Abner. "That 'girl!' Why, Miss Gertie's old as you are, isn't she?"

It was Cornwall's turn to chuckle. "As old as your grandpa, anyhow. Listen, Three. Get ready to hold your nose all day tomorrow—and the next day, too."

"Why?" Three asked, surprised.

"Well, that old Abner is going to put you to work on giving Ragwing her two coats of airplane dope. And does that stuff *stink!*"

"Won't you be helping, too?"

"Nope. I'll be tinkerin' with this motor. But don't worry—I'll be holdin' my nose!"

Two days later, the great decision was made.

Abner, stroking the final coat of clear airplane dope over Ragwing's patched sides, noticed that the old wrangler and Three were working like a team on Ragwing's motor. "Cornwall's not 'uneasy' with Three anymore. Must be because Three told him last night that he was a pretty good cook. And I bet Three would hate to remember he ever said to Cornwall, 'you can carry my suitcase.'"

He stepped back to look at the plane. "She's starting to look like the old Ragwing," he called out proudly. "Now if we can just get the bird to fly! I'd say we're about ready to try her out. What do you think, Cornwall?"

Cornwall and Three walked over. Cornwall sighed. "Ready as she'll ever be—which ain't saying much." He turned to Three. "What d'you think?"

Three tried to look thoughtful instead of proud. His opinion had been asked! He looked Ragwing over. "Hmm. Well—sure. Sure."

"Then it's settled," Abner said. "Tomorrow's the big day."

Three nearly bounced off the barn floor. "Gee, I wish the kids from school could be here!"

Cornwall and Abner flashed a quick glance at each other, and a sad look came into the eyes of both old men.

When they rolled Ragwing out of the barn the next morning, she managed to look cheerful as a hummingbird with the gleaming new coat of clear airplane dope stroked over her patched sides. Three trotted around to the cockpit.

"Hey!" Abner called. "Wait a minute, Son. Where do you think you're going?"

Three's eyes widened in surprise. "With you, Abner."

"Three, this is just a test. All I'm going to do is taxi her along the ground. See how she handles, y'know."

Three stared. "But you said *we*—you *promised*."

"I promised to take you up when it was safe. I'm not sure it's safe, and I'm *not* going to fly. Okay? Besides," he added quickly, "*we* means the ground crew. You don't hear Cornwall complaining, do you?"

"Okay," Three replied, disappointment in his voice.

"Then get ready to pull the chocks from the wheels when I holler." Abner climbed into the cockpit and shouted down to Cornwall, "Okay! Powder River! Let 'er buck!"

Cornwall took hold of the propeller blade. "Contact?"

"Contact!"

Ragwing's motor chirped, hollered, gave a most unbirdlike belch, and died out.

"Try again!" Abner shouted. "Contact!"

This time Ragwing gave a few chokes, splutters, then settled into a kind of unsteady roar. Abner grinned, hunched over, and yelled out, "Chocks!"

Cornwall stepped aside, Three pulled away the

chocks, and Abner gave a wave. Ragwing started on a wobbly trek along the driveway.

"Cornwall," Three asked, as he watched Ragwing's progress, "do you think he's really going to take me up?"

Cornwall suddenly looked extra-interested in the plane. "Come on, Three. Let's take a jog after her. We want to watch careful-like, don't we?"

By the time they made it to the end of the drive, Abner was already swinging Ragwing into the deserted highway.

Behind his old World War I goggles, his eyes sparkled as Ragwing responded to his touch and picked up speed. The gleaming little plane leaped forward faster and faster. The tail leveled up from the ground, and she stretched out gracefully toward the up-sloping ribbon of concrete ahead.

"Look at her go!" Cornwall exclaimed as they watched Ragwing zoom up the road.

Then a terrifying sight appeared. On the crest of the hill ahead, an enormous truck came careening along, black against the blue sky.

Cornwall's face froze.

Three looked stunned.

Only Abner acted. For an instant a vision of death in the skies of France swirled before his eyes. Then suddenly Abner was no longer an old man. Every quick reaction of those Baron von Richthofen days came back. *When you can't go under or around—go over!* With a prayer on his lips, he pulled back on the stick.

As the truck thundered down the hill, Ragwing started her rise. Up! Up! And at the last possible moment she swept off the concrete, and with

wheels almost grazing the truck's top, she roared into the sky.

Sassy as a jaybird, the little patched-up plane began to circle back toward Three and Cornwall. Abner couldn't resist it. "WAAAHOO!" he yelled from the cockpit.

He whizzed over the two standing below. Then with a friendly waggling dip of wings, he went cruising low over the barn and farmhouse.

Suddenly a cold draft of air hit his legs and the happy grin on his face faded fast. He tried to look down to see what was causing the inrush of air.

Down on the drive and running at top speed, Cornwall had no trouble in spotting danger. A whole flap of patching had ripped off—and the triangle was getting bigger every second as the wind tore into the fuselage.

"LAND, Abner! LAND!" Cornwall shouted at the top of his lungs.

Three saw another flap go. "She's coming apart!" he screamed.

She was—and like a peeled banana. Blue sky was beginning to show plainly through Ragwing's tail section.

Abner swooped downward for a landing. In the steep glide, even more linen ripped away. By now he looked as though he were piloting a glider.

"A plucked chicken!" Cornwall groaned. "He's headin' for the highway again. Let's go!"

"Faith and hope," he gasped, beginning to run, with Three leading the chase.

"He's landed!" Three yelled. "He's safe!"

Almost as he said it, Ragwing veered from the center of the highway, and although Abner desperately fought the controls, the propeller splintered its way along the farm fencing. Then the skeleton tail section tilted high in the air. Slowly, Ragwing settled back. The motor cut off.

A deadly silence settled over the wreck.

It took help from both Cornwall and Three to get Abner out of the cockpit. He had a bleeding cut on his forehead and he looked a little dazed.

Cornwall helped him to sag down on a nearby boulder.

"You all right, Abner?" Three panted.

"Sure he's all right," Cornwall said anxiously. "Ain't you, Abner?"

Abner smiled shakily. "Fit as a fiddle any second now." He looked at Three. "If the Red Baron couldn't get me, no rickety fence is going to. How's Ragwing?"

"I hate to say," Cornwall shuddered. "Let's just get her back to the barn."

It was late afternoon before Ragwing, tattered and torn, was under shelter.

"We can fix her—can't we?" Three asked.

Abner was afraid to look at Cornwall. He knew how much Cornwall had disapproved of the project right from the start. He hesitated. "Well—sure we can, Son. We've a spare propeller somewhere around here, and we both know Cornwall is a wizard with engines."

Cornwall waved his hand in the air. "Now you just hold on, Abner. I agreed *once* to help, but—"

Abner leaned forward to inspect the damaged plane, and reached in his pocket for his glasses.

"Now how do you like that?" He held them up to the light. "Cracked. Both sides. Three, run up to the house, will you, and get my other pair? They're on the table right beside my bed."

As Three sped off, Cornwall shook his head at Abner. "This old crate ain't never goin' to fly again. You know it, Abner. Who do you think you're kiddin'?"

Abner began to putter with the engine. "Oh, I don't know," he said easily. "Maybe. Maybe not. But I'm not going to quit on her too quickly." He glanced toward the house. "Or quit on Three, either," he added.

Cornwall angrily slapped his wide-brimmed hat against Ragwing's nose. "Dang it, Abner. I know how you feel about the boy. But that don't mean you gotta kill yourself all because he wants to take a sky ride."

There was no reply.

"How about some *land* ridin' for a change? Maybe I could get him interested in ridin' my horse," Cornwall went on. "It's a sight closer to the ground from a saddle than from a cockpit, ain't it?"

Abner straightened up. "Wonder how long it's going to take Three to get my specs?"

Cornwall sighed. "I give up," he said gloomily, and stalked out of the barn.

Three hurried over to the night table by Abner's bed. The glasses case rested on top of a stack of letters. "This is sure turning into a better vacation than I thought," he said to himself, snatching up the case.

Then he suddenly noticed the top letter. There in the top corner was the same Wakefield crest as the one on his blazer pocket. And there, plain as day, was the address—Abner Therman.

"Why, it's my letter!" he exclaimed in amazement. "What's it doing here?"

He turned it over and saw the back flap had been opened. He hesitated. "It must be mine. Nobody at Wakefield would be writing to Abner."

Still holding the glasses case, he shook the letter out. *"It is mine, and Abner opened my mail!"*

He began to read.

Dear Three:

I'm glad you left your grandfather's address with me, as I certainly want you to know how sorry I am that your father decided to take you out of Wakefield Academy. We will all miss you—and especially Billy Norton. . . .

Three could read no more. It seemed to him that the whole world had fallen apart. His voice was a choked whisper. "And Abner knew it all the time, and he didn't even *tell* me. And he didn't have any *right* to open my letter." He flung the glasses case on the bed and, snatching up the letter, ran to his room.

The kitchen door slammed. "Three!" Abner called. "Where the heck are my specs?"

There was no reply.

Puzzled, Abner walked into the hallway and into Three's bedroom.

The story was all there—the Wakefield letter on the bed, Levis, shirt, boots, and the beloved Stetson flung around the room. Abner crossed to the closet.

The hangers that once held a pair of gray flannel trousers and a blue Wakefield Academy blazer, now hung empty. Abner's glance went to the floor. The black shoes that Three had so carefully polished after his adventure on the tractor were gone, too.

Abner charged out of the room and on out to the porch. "Three!" he shouted. "Three! Where are you? I want to talk to you!"

In the warm yellow light of late afternoon, there was no answering cry. Only the hum of insects and a few lazy trills of birdsong broke the stillness.

Abner Therman III was gone.

CHAPTER 7

"I hate to do it," Abner said, "but I guess I'd better call the police. I drove halfway into town and didn't see hide nor hair of him. He must have hitched a ride."

Cornwall nodded. "Guess so. I've given this place a good goin'-over. Not a sign of him."

The phone rang. Abner hurried to it.

"Abner?" a low voice said. "Grimes—here at the airport. Listen, Abner. I've got your grandson here. He wants to fly to San Francisco. He had the money for a ticket, and I sold one to him. Then I got to thinking. I thought—well, I thought I'd better call you."

Abner nearly exploded. When he stopped talking, Grimes' voice crackled over the wire. "Hold it, Abner. I did call you, didn't I? But okay. I'll keep him here. I won't let him get on that flight."

From the bench just outside Grimes' office, Three heard every word through the open window above him. "I'm *not* going back to that farm," he muttered. "But I'd better get out of here *fast*."

Just then, Ben, the postmaster, came whirling up in his red, white and blue mail truck. He hurried inside the building with a small sack of mail. Three looked around. There were only two other persons waiting for the plane, and they seemed to be paying no attention to anything but the sky. Walking slowly, and doing nothing that would attract their attention, Three wandered over to the mail truck. Making sure nobody was watching, he hopped in and crawled to the back. "Sure hope he doesn't look back here," he muttered, as he scrunched himself into a corner.

He heard approaching footsteps. The door opened and slammed. The motor started. Ben hadn't spotted him!

"You promised me you'd watch him!" Abner nearly shouted at Grimes. His face was lined with worry.

"Abner, I *did* watch him—until the plane came in. Then I had to go out there. You know that. But I swear only two passengers got on. That's it."

Cornwall looked around. "Then if he didn't get on the plane, he couldn't have gone far in this time. Maybe he hitched a ride back to town. Was anybody here who'd give him a lift?"

"Not a soul," Grimes said. "Wait! Ben and his mail truck."

Abner didn't waste time saying goodbye. He hurried out to the truck, and with Cornwall hanging on for dear life, headed for town and for Ben's front door.

"Abner," Ben pleaded. "Don't you think I know the difference between a boy and a mail sack? I just parked the truck at the post office, and walked on home, per usual."

"And you're *sure* Three wasn't hiding there in the back?"

"Didn't look. Why should I? The mail was all delivered. You don't think I'd leave valuable government property in a parked truck, do you? Listen, Abner—I'm not going to stand here all night. I'm missing the Late, Late Show. I'm sorry about Three, but that's it."

"He didn't take a plane," Cornwall said, as they got back into the truck. "And we know he didn't take a train—cause it don't stop here."

Abner's hand slapped down on the steering wheel. "How stupid can we be! Three just hopped out of that mail truck and went over to the bus stop at Cholly's Cafe. Let's go."

"If I'd known he was your grandson, Abner," Cholly said, "I wouldn't have sold him a ticket. But that bus has got an awful big head start on you. Better call the police chief. He could catch up, maybe, sooner than you could."

"Not the way I'll drive!" Abner answered grimly.

Cornwall groaned as he stepped back into the truck. "Sure wish you'd get seat belts installed in this here wagon. I tell you, Abner, if you drive too fast, my boots are goin' to go plumb through the floorboards."

Cornwall didn't need to worry. They weren't three miles out from town when the Chief's prowl car came looming up, lights flashing. "So it's you, Abner Therman," the Chief said in a pleased voice when he walked up to the window. "You must think you can walk right through my fresh paint or burn up the State's highway—anything your little heart desires." He pulled out his ticket pad.

"Now just you hold on!" Abner exclaimed. "I'm catching up with the San Francisco bus. Have to do it before it gets to the next town. My grandson's on it."

"Is that so?" The Chief licked the tip of his pencil. "Well, you can't do it. So that's that."

Cornwall could see that Abner's temper was building up higher and higher. "Maybe you'd catch 'em, Chief?—bein' as you're the Law?"

"Out of my territory. We're not a half mile from the County line," the Chief said, looking pleased.

"Why *you*—!" Abner nearly choked.

"Cornwall," the Chief ordered, "you slide behind the wheel and follow us back to town. Abner's riding with me."

"I'm a dangerous criminal, I suppose," Abner said bitterly as he settled into the prowl car. "I explained why I was in a hurry."

"There's no need to go on about it," the Chief replied, as he made a U-turn and swung back toward town. "You're dangerous driving so fast. Trouble with you amateurs, you come running to us experts too late. Why didn't you call me right away? I'd have—"

"I haven't called you yet," Abner replied angrily. "And would you mind too much turning off that siren? We're almost back at the farm, and I want to *think*."

"Okay, Abner." The Chief turned off the switch. "But your thinking ain't going to help. What this case needs is *pros*—not two old galoots tromping over all the clues."

He zoomed on through the town's main street and headed for Abner's farm.

As the police car, followed by the farm truck, swung up into the driveway, the porch light snapped on and Gertie came out.

"What's all the commotion?" she asked, as the men stepped out into the yard.

"No time for questions now, Gert," the Chief said importantly. "I've a missing-persons case on my hands—Abner's grandson."

Gertie eyed him coldly. "That so? Well let me give you a clue, Chief. Abner's grandson is in his bed and fast asleep—unless your flashing around all over waked him up."

The Chief looked like a balloon rapidly losing air. He turned to Abner. "If this is one of your durn-fool stunts—"

But even the Chief knew from the expression of relief on Abner's face, that this hadn't been a stunt. Grumpily, he marched off to the prowl car. "About what I expected," he said, sliding behind the wheel. "Another false alarm." And with a fresh long wail on the siren, he whizzed off down the driveway.

"Cheering up himself and the cows, I suspect." Gertie said briskly. "Now, Abner, you needn't explain anything. I got the story straight from Three. Found him standing in front of Cholly's Cafe. He'd missed the bus and was waiting for the next. So I coaxed him home with me for dinner."

She stopped and looked coldly at Cornwall. "You should have seen the boy eat. Doubt if he's had a decent meal since he's been here."

Cornwall glared, but made no reply.

"Anyhow," Gertie went on, "I heard his side of the story. He thinks you opened his mail, or even if you didn't do it on purpose, you didn't tell him about it. Well, he's got it in his head that his dad is too busy for anything but business, and neither one of you cares if he goes back to that school or not. Anyhow, he was going to have it out with his dad one way or another. So I said, 'Since your father is so busy, maybe he isn't even in San Francisco. You'd better use my phone and call him first before you start out.' " She paused. "Well, Two was in Seattle, so I coaxed Three to let me bring him back here for the night anyhow. But fact of the matter is—he doesn't *have* any place to go—I mean, where he wants to be."

There was a silence. Gertie spoke up again. "He'd have a great place to *stay*, though. Right here. All we have to do is make him understand *somebody* really cares about him. I mean—somebody is honest with him. That school wouldn't be so important to him if you could do that, Abner." She hesitated. "But I just would like to have you know that I did stick up for you."

Abner sighed. "I always can count on you, Gertie. I know that. Thanks a lot. Want me to drive you back home? That old car of yours looks as though it might break down any minute."

Gertie's chin went up. "That car is *young*. So no thanks. Besides, there's something I'm going to take a look at before I leave this place—that contraption in the barn you've had Three all excited about."

"Contraption!" Cornwall gasped. "That there is no 'contraption.' It so happens it's one of the few 1920's biplanes in maybe the whole world—accordin' to Three, anyhow."

Under the strung-up lights, Gertie stared at Ragwing's tattered outline—a sad sight, but it brought no tears to her eyes. "Abner, this is the biggest pile of junk I've ever seen in my life."

She scowled and stared from Abner to Cornwall. Then she dropped her bombshell. "What I want to know is—how are we ever going to make her fly?"

Abner and Cornwall looked stunned. "Fly! Who said anything about flying?"

"I did," Gertie snapped. "Abner Therman, haven't you been listening to me? You may not know it, but that boy thinks the world of you. And you, too, Cornwall. Trouble is—"

"I know what the trouble is, Gert," Abner said grimly. "He thinks I've double-crossed him. Opened his mail and wrecked Ragwing—maybe on purpose."

"*Poof!*" Gertie exclaimed. "I doubt that very much. But right this minute, you and Cornwall should be working on this wretched flying machine. And I might be just dumb enough to help you put her together."

Cornwall shuddered. "*You!*"

"Me," Gertie snapped. She stared at both of them. "How'd *you* like to have to spend a whole, long summer with nobody put two old codgers like you?"

Abner and Cornwall blinked. "Been doing just that for a long time," Abner replied.

Cornwall eyed Gertie. "Way you been talkin', Gertie, guess you mean *three* old codgers, don't you?"

Gertie gasped. "Speak for yourself, Cornwall,"

she answered tartly. "Well, *I* shall say goodnight as you two seem to be in no mood to go to work."

She started for the barn door. "Expect me in the morning—*early*," she called over her shoulder.

Cornwall exploded. "Expect her in the mornin' —early! There now, Abner! See the trouble you got us into now? Told you all along we should've dragged the crate to the dump."

CHAPTER 8

A bright, sunny morning wasn't helping Three to feel cheerful. "One thing worse than running away is getting back," he muttered gloomily, as he tied the laces of his Wakefield shoes. He looked sadly toward his Stetson hat. "Probably I'll never wear that again. Abner's going to be mad at me and when Dad hears what I did, he'll be even madder. Oh, well. I'd better go out and get the whole thing over with."

He walked down the hall and through the kitchen without even stopping to put together a peanut butter and jelly sandwich.

From the barn came the sound of a sanding machine, and to Three's surprise, Miss Gertie's old car was parked nearby. He groaned. *"Everybody's* there, and I'll have to go around saying how sorry I am when about the only thing I'm sorry about is just being here."

As he stepped through the barn doorway, Cornwall switched off the sander. "Had your breakfast?" he asked.

"There are fresh strawberries in the refrigerator," Miss Gertie said. "Brought them over this morning."

"And there's French toast in the oven," Cornwall announced. He glared at Miss Gertie. "Mighty *good* French toast."

Abner ripped off a torn piece of linen from the fuselage. "When you finish your breakfast, Three, you'd better change into your American clothes. We're going to need all the help we can get out here."

Three couldn't believe his ears. "You mean you're going to rebuild it—I mean, her?"

"I promised to take you flying, didn't I?" Abner grinned.

If Cornwall and Miss Gertie hadn't been standing right there, Three would have *run* to Abner. Instead, he said, stiffly, "I'll hurry, Sir. Back right away, Sir."

"I'm going to sew a new linen skin for Ragwing," Gertie called out to him. "I'll show you tonight when you all come over to my place."

Cornwall groaned loudly and turned the sanding machine back on.

Gertie's living room was draped with large and small pieces of linen in just about every color Three had ever seen. And on the carpet Abner was spreading out the old cracked patterns of Ragwing's fuselage.

"Turn on the TV, if you want to, Three," Gertie called from across the room. "Looks to me like matching up these linen pieces to Abner's patterns is going to take some figuring."

She turned to Abner. "I wish you'd let me order some natural color linen for you, Abner, instead of using all these leftovers."

Abner, down on his hands and knees smoothing

out the patterns, shook his head. "Don't want to wait that long. Besides, a little color won't hurt."

"A little color! This plane's going to look like Joseph's coat."

"No matter," Abner replied. "Cutting and stitching all this stuff together for us—why you're a treasure, my love." He got to his feet and gave Gertie a grateful kiss.

Cornwall looked as though he wished he were out riding the lonesome prairie. He turned his head quickly to the TV where a horde of Indians rode silently across the screen.

"How do you get the sound on, Miss Gertie?" Three called over. "I don't know what's going on."

Miss Gertie looked up. "You *don't?*" She watched the screen for a moment. "I do. Now let's see. The Chief has threatened to go to war because Black Bart stole his land. I imagine that cowboy the Chief is talking to is Black Bart's brother, and he's promising to help the Chief get his land back."

Cornwall stared at the screen and nodded solemnly.

Gertie suddenly changed to a low, growling voice. "We have always wanted peace with white man. But white man does not want peace."

She switched to a good-guy voice. "Works two ways, Chief. Strike back at a few no-good, murderin' white men and you'd turn the frontier into a needless war."

Away galloped the cowboy as Gertie sang out, "Cloppity, cloppity, cloppity."

Before the program ended, even Cornwall had gotten into the spirit of the thing, and was blowing unseen smoke from his unseen six-shooter, and

Three was choking with laughter at Gertie's antics. "I'll do the commercial," he volunteered.

"Let me," Abner chuckled. He stood up. "Folks, you're all invited to take part in the next marvellous program going on in Miss Gertie Spencer's living room——Mission Ragwing."

Gertie giggled. "Say no more, Mr. Announcer. We can take a hint."

Getting Ragwing in take-off shape was no small job. If it hadn't been for Gertie's sewing, plus her speedy organization of a larger ground crew, the little biplane might never have been rolled out of the barn.

But with Abner and Cornwall heading up the job, and the best efforts of Three, Gertie, Ben, the Postmaster, and Cholly, the cafe owner, it began to look as though the bird would fly—and soon. Ragwing was turning into a patchwork doll.

"We ought to have a christening party," Gertie said at the end of a third night's hard work. "How about tomorrow, Abner? Think she'll be ready?"

"Don't see why not," Abner replied. "We can give her the final coat of airplane dope—"

"And then we can finally stop holding our noses," Three added.

"A christening party is on," Miss Gertie crowed. "I'll supply the picnic. And, Cornwall, you can string up some paper lanterns around this barn. Wouldn't want you to go to a lot of bother cooking." She hastily said goodnight before Cornwall could think up an answer that suited him.

"I'll get out my camera and take pictures,"

Three said. "I sure want to send some to Billy Norton. He's never going to believe just *telling* about it—a real, *flyable* plane over fifty years old!"

A sudden thought hit him. "And that makes my best friends over *seventy!* I guess I just won't mention that to Billy. He'd never understand."

Seventy, seventeen, or seven, it was the best party Three had ever imagined. Gertie's picnic was wonderful, and Cholly had contributed a whole case of cokes. Even Cornwall was so pleased that he took a mouth organ from his pocket and furnished music for dancing. Gertie, the belle of the ball, was breathless after doing an Irish jig with Abner. "You know," she panted, "we've forgotten one thing."

"What's that?" Abner asked.

"The christening. Here Cholly's got Ragwing's name all newly painted and nobody's christened her. Three, hand me that coke bottle."

Three handed her the bottle with one hand and picked up his camera with the other. "This'll make a great shot," he said excitedly.

Gertie took a firm grip on the neck of the bottle, and swung hard. Three's flash brightened the scene. But Ragwing wasn't christened—yet. The bottle didn't even crack. Instantly, Gertie was showered with advice from everyone. "Now swing again, Gert," Abner said. "Put some muscle in it, girl!"

Gertie drew back her arm, paused, then swung forward with all her might. POW! Three's camera recorded the strangest view of a christening ever

on film—Gertie's wrist! Somewhere under Ragwing's bright new patching, were the christening
bottle and her hand.

"HOLY SMOKE, Gert!" Cornwall yelled.
"What did you go and do that for?"

"Mercy!" Gertie gasped. "Cornwall, I never
meant—. Why 'sakes'!" She looked about to cry.

"Well, I guess you ain't done the damage you
think," Cornwall said in a kinder voice. "You ain't
hurt your hand, and that hole can be patched
again." His voice turned sad. "Only a few more
hours work—that's all."

"You couldn't beat it for a real first-class chris-
tening," Abner said. "Don't you worry your head,
Gert. We'll have her fixed in no time. Three and
I will do it first thing in the morning."

Ragwing's newest patch did nothing but add to
her already cheerful look, and by mid-morning she
was ready for her motor test.

Three looked hopefully up to the cockpit. "Abner, can I go with you this time?"

"Hop in," Abner replied. "Why not?"

Cornwall, beside the propeller, peered around
up to the cockpit. "Contact?" he called.

Abner nodded to Three. "Better tell him," he
said, grinning.

"CONTACT!" Three roared out.

Cornwall gave the prop a mighty heave and
quickly stepped back from the whirling blades.
The motor roared to life. But the satisfied look on
Cornwall's face suddenly faded. Ragwing's roar
was turning to an ominous *clank* that was growing
louder every second.

Cornwall swung up his hands. "Abner! Cut the motor!"

Too late! There was a loud metallic CRACK! Ragwing shook from nose to rudder as smoke poured out of the cowling. There was a gut-churning grinding sound followed by awful silence as Abner turned off the ignition. Hurriedly he reached for the fire extinguisher. "Get out, Three. Jump!"

White clouds covered the motor as Abner used the extinguisher.

"What happened to her?" Three asked unbelievingly as they gathered around Ragwing's motor. "She started just fine."

Cornwall shook his head. "Just like I said. Old metal. It crystallized. Abner, what you need now is a miracle—or a new motor."

Abner's shoulders drooped. "They haven't made these motors since before World War II."

Three turned away. Abner and Cornwall said no more until the rear door of the barn shut and Three disappeared from sight. Then Cornwall sighed. "If I was you, Abner, I'd give up. Look's as though Three has."

Abner stared at the wrecked motor. He straightened up. "No. I promised him a ride and he's going to get it—one way or another."

But Cornwall wasn't listening. He grabbed Abner's arm, forcing him to turn toward the barn entrance. "D'you see what I see!" he exclaimed excitedly. He pointed.

Turning in from the highway was the rented VW. Abner sprang into action. "Hurry up! Get those barn doors closed. If Two sees Ragwing we'll *all* be grounded!"

They rushed to the entrance. Cornwall grabbed one door and Abner the other. Cornwall slid the holding bar into place. Together they strolled slowly toward the house to greet Abner Therman II.

CHAPTER 9

"Hi!" Two called out. He brought the VW to a stop by the porch.

"Thought you were in Seattle," Abner said as Two stepped from the car.

"I was," Two replied. He turned to Cornwall. "How's the cooking around here these days?" But he didn't wait for an answer. "Where's Three?" he asked. "I had a change in schedule, and I don't have to be back in the office until tomorrow morning, so I flew down to see him."

"Tomorrow mornin'!" Cornwall exclaimed. "Now ain't that fine—it bein' no more'n afternoon now." He turned his back on the newcomer and marched off into the house.

Abner Two stared briefly at Cornwall's back then turned to his father. "Where is Three?"

"Behind the barn, maybe," Abner replied. "Anyhow, you can be sure he didn't see you drive up. A few days ago he even tried to run away to see you."

"You're kidding!"

Abner shook his head. "You know that school means a lot to him, Two. But the boy needs you more than Wakefield or that new place you got picked out for him. Now, if I were you—"

Two cut in. "Okay, Dad. Okay. I'll talk to him —not that I don't appreciate your advice."

Abner half-smiled. "Didn't know as how I'd given any—yet."

Two looked at his father sharply. "Guess you didn't. But I'm the one who has to handle this."

Abner looked at his son. Then almost under his breath, said, "Hope you can."

"What'd you say, Dad?"

Abner shrugged. "Why don't you look for Three back of the barn. I'm going on into the house."

When his father rounded the corner of the barn, Three was jackknifed into an old tire that hung from a tree bough.

"Hi, Three!"

"Hi," Three said, not getting up.

His father frowned. "How's life here at old Crummybrook farm?"

Three shoved a heel into the packed earth and started the tire swinging. "Okay."

His father smiled. "You know, this is a family tire tree. Your grandfather hung one here for me years ago." He laughed. "The tree's grown some since."

Three made no reply.

"What's wrong, Son?" Abner Two asked. "Let's have it."

Three stared at him for a moment, "Dad, I want to talk about going back to school. I mean—going back to Wakefield."

Abner Two shook his head. "Wish you'd had the news from me first, but I've been so—"

"Busy," Three said, flatly. "I know."

His father scowled. "Don't you realize that if you're in a school close to San Francisco we'll be able to spend weekends together?"

Three nodded. "Sure. That is, when you're in town."

"I won't be traveling so much anymore," his father said.

Three stepped out of the tire swing. "You say that, Dad. But then on Friday nights you'll call from some weird town and say, 'sorry, I can't make it.'"

Before his father could reply, Three brushed past him and went on to the farmhouse.

Cornwall did his best during dinner to keep the conversation going. But none of the three Abners helped much.

"Got one more piece of pie," Cornwall said. "Want it, Three?"

"No, thank you." Three stood up. "Excuse me, please. I think I'll turn in."

Cornwall was the next to leave. He looked from Abner to his son, and said, "Guess I'd better go out and check the barn."

Left alone, Two looked at his father. "Go ahead. Fire your best shots. You won't hurt my feelings."

Abner looked down at his coffee cup. "Well— way I see it, as far as the boy is concerned, you've only got one choice." He paused. "Two, settle down. Make an honest-to-Pete real home for him and for you, too. You have to start in by finding a house in a nice neighborhood with a lot of kids, near a good old-fashioned public school."

Two looked thoughtful. "This may sound crazy to you, Dad, but ever since Three's mother died—well, I've had this thing against buying a house. Minute I do, and walk through that door, then I'll *know* she won't be there—ever."

Abner's eyes looked kindly at his own boy. "I know that feeling, Son. I felt the same way when I lost your mother." He swallowed before he could begin again. "But I've always wished I could have looked a fact in the face. Maybe if I had, you wouldn't be chasing around the world wearing yourself out. You'd be here—making a good life for you and for Three."

Two put down his fork. "You didn't do so badly, Dad. Wish I'd have done as well. I'll start by taking Three back with me tomorrow. I can shift my work around. I'll take him down to San Diego, maybe. We can take a look at the zoo, there. I guess I have to start getting re-acquainted with my own boy. He's been a real chore for you. I know that. Running away—and all that stuff. But don't worry. He'll leave with me in the morning."

Abner quietly slipped inside the barn door. Cornwall was looking at the damaged Ragwing.

"How did it go?" he asked.

"Pretty good," Abner replied. "I got him all steamed up about buying a house and settling down. Trouble is—he wants to take Three back with him in the morning."

"What's wrong with that?" Cornwall asked.

Abner shook his head. "Doesn't fit in with my plans. I had it all figured out. Three was going on my last flight. My farewell appearance, you might say."

Cornwall tilted back his hat. "Abner, it's only an airplane, for goodness' sake!"

Abner looked him in the eye. "That's *only* a horse you got out in the corral. But how would you feel if you had to give up that one last ride *for good?* Anyhow, I promised the boy, and I have to think of something."

The two old men switched off the barn lights and walked outside. "This ain't the only plane in the world, Abner," Cornwall said. "Why don't you rent one and take Three up?"

Abner shook his head. "I'd have to have my papers in order. I'd never pass a physical—much less the eye test." He sighed heavily. "Well, come on. Might as well close the barn doors and call it a day."

The two old-timers walked slowly toward the house. Abner stared up at the Big Dipper. "There must be some place where we can get a motor," he muttered.

"Pretty late for that," Cornwall replied gloomily.

"Maybe I could call that Harley man in town. Call him at his house, I mean," Abner said. "If—" Suddenly he grabbed Cornwall's arm. "Wait!"

"What's the matter?" Cornwall asked in alarm.

"Look, Cornwall. Over there!" He pointed to the rented Volkswagen that Two had left parked near the porch. "It doesn't amount to much. Thirty-six horsepower. But it's air-cooled, and—" He flung his arms wide. "Of course! Why, sure!"

Cornwall stared. "Abner, what on earth you talkin' about?"

Abner went striding toward the little car, Cornwall at his heels. "That VW engine, of course. I read all about it in *Science and Mechanics*. It's more horses than we need, but—"

"*We* need!" Cornwall nearly jumped off the ground. "WE!"

"Keep your voice down, Cornwall," Abner said calmly. "No need to tell the whole countryside what we're going to do."

Cornwall rolled his eyes toward the stars. "Abner Therman, I'm warnin' you now. I never been no horse thief nor engine thief neither. And I don't aim to start now."

"Who said anything about stealing?" Abner chuckled. "We're just going to *borrow* it."

Cornwall tugged at his ear. "I don't like it, Abner."

"You get on that side and I'll get on this," Abner said. "Come on now, Cornwall. PUSH."

"Lucky there ain't no moon tonight," Cornwall panted, as they heaved the VW safely forward into the shelter of the dark barn. "I'd feel like a danged fool if I'd abeen caught pussyfootin' around in our own backyard. Talk about stealin' hub caps! Can't tell *me* this ain't wrong." He wiped his forehead with a polka-dot bandanna. "We're breakin' the law—pure and simple."

"Cornwall, will you kindly stop saying the same thing fifty-two different ways and turn on the lights?"

"And close the barn door first," Cornwall growled.

Doors closed and lights on, Abner stood back in satisfaction. "Now let's get going with the block and tackle. We'll be lucky if we get two hours' sleep before morning. There's a lot to do here."

Hours later, Abner and Cornwall stood back to admire Ragwing. She gleamed bright and sassy under the barn lights.

"Well, that's that," Cornwall heaved a sigh. "And danged if I feel like just plain goin' to bed. I've half a mind to call Gertie for a second chrisenin'."

For the first time, Abner looked uncertain. "Do you think it will work?"

"Think it will work! Why, of course it will work. Didn't I do just what the book said? Not right on the nose. Thirty-three hundred rpm. But close. Very close."

"Well this is no time to take risks," Abner replied worriedly.

Cornwall's jaw dropped. "Risks! Comin' from you that's some speech!"

Abner nodded. "Guess so. Well, let's push the Volks back where it was and turn in."

"Couldn't push it in the mornin', could we?" Cornwall asked. "I ain't sleepy. Just half-dead, that's all."

"You don't want to get arrested before breakfast, do you? We'll put it back so Two won't notice his transportation's come up missing. Cornwall—" he hesitated.

"Yep?"

"Thanks."

"Tweren't nothin'."

CHAPTER 10

Pink light shimmered over the barn roof and the silent farmhouse when Three, carrying his sneakers, softly closed the porch door behind him.

"Where's Abner?" he whispered to Cornwall, who sat on the porch steps warming his hands around a steaming coffee mug.

Cornwall turned around. "Right behind you," he grinned.

Three looked back and nearly dropped the sneakers. *"Abner!* Why—why—you look like a real flying ace!"

"I was," Abner grinned. He was dressed in his old leather jacket, flying helmet with goggles pushed up, and was winding a long silk scarf around his neck.

He handed Three a helmet, goggles, and scarf. Then, with a kind of gruff dignity, he took a set of World War I Wings from his pocket and held them out to Three.

"Were those *yours?"* Three's voice was nearly a whisper.

Abner nodded and pinned them on Three's plaid shirt. "I earned them," the old man said proudly. "Now they're yours, Three. Wear them in pride."

He took out a slender strip of red silk and fastened it to the back of Three's helmet. "And this is my old banderole. It will fly in the slipstream."

Cornwall shook his head. "If you two drugstore pilots don't get goin'—it's gonna be all quiet on the Western Front today. And that's for sure."

They all glanced back at the house where Abner Two was still peacefully dreaming—they hoped.

"Gosh," Three muttered as he strode to the barn with Abner and Cornwall. "I feel like I'm on a combat mission. Wonder how I ought to tie this scarf?"

Abner solved that problem just before he climbed into the cockpit. "Learning to tie one of these things was about all they had time to teach us before sending us up to fight in the old days."

Cornwall went to Ragwing's propeller. "You two keep admirin' yourselves, and gettin' that scarf tied is about all you'll get to do today."

Bursting with excitement, Three climbed into the rear cockpit behind Abner.

"Fasten your seat belt, Three."

Cornwall peered forward impatiently. "Contact?" he called out.

"CONTACT!" Three yelled back.

Ragwing's motor barked loudly, then stopped. In the silence of the morning, the bark sounded like an explosion, and in his bedroom Abner Two sat up. "Must be dynamiting somewhere," he thought sleepily, and fell back against the pillow.

Out in the barn, Cornwall put every bit of strength he had in giving the prop a second heave. The VW engine roared to life—and held!

Abner Two leaped out of bed and rushed to the window. *"Oh, no!"* he gasped, staring at the open barn doors. "He *wouldn't!"*

Grabbing his robe and slippers he left the bedroom at top speed.

Too late! Abner had slammed the throttle home. Ragwing was on the move! And she came bursting out into the sunlight!

Bo barked deliriously. Mabel honked a wild salute before waddling off to safety at top speed. Abner Two came exploding out of the kitchen door, waving his green-striped pajama sleeves wildly as he tried to head off the oncoming Ragwing. But nothing was going to stop her steady taxiing run along the drive, and Two dropped face down in the dirt just in time. Ragwing's wings streaked over his head.

Cornwall came running behind the plane. "Mornin'," he called calmly, as he galloped past Two.

Two leaped to his feet. *"Morning?"* he shouted, springing up after Cornwall. "Is everybody crazy around here? What's everybody *doing?"*

Cornwall didn't bother to reply. He watched Ragwing wheel into the highway, and skim along the concrete until her wheels cleared the paving.

Abner pulled back on the stick. Ragwing rose like a joyous bird. Cornwall waved, Abner and Three waved back—and Two stood frozen, his hands at his sides, his brain not quite getting the message his eyes were sending.

Abner and Three each grinned. "Might as well give 'em a real show," Abner shouted. "Okay?"

Gracefully, Ragwing made a banking left turn,

and came gliding back high over the farm. Then, before Abner Two's horrified eyes, his father executed a perfect loop-the-loop, and gaily buzzed off.

Two ran to his VW, slamming the door and turning the ignition key in almost one motion. "I've got to get help!" But there was no help from the VW—not even the whining sound of a dead battery. He leaped out and lifted the hood. *"I don't believe it!"*

He spotted Cornwall ambling back up the drive. "My motor's missing," he yelled. "I mean *really* missing! You've stolen it!"

Cornwall's pleased expression didn't change. "Borrowed it," he replied sweetly. "We'll give it back."

High in the sky, Abner and Three viewed the earth below and the clouds above. "WHooee!" Abner shouted. Should have done this years ago! Powder River—"

"LET HER BUCK!" Three yelled forward.

Abner dipped, swerved, and made a perfect pass back over the farmhouse.

Even Cornwall, listening in disapproval as Two talked on the phone to the police chief, ducked low when Ragwing made her swing over the farmhouse roof.

"I said," Two shouted again, "I don't want him arrested, Chief. I just want you to get help. I want him protected when he tries to land."

There was another roaring swoop overhead as Ragwing made a second pass. Abner Two's voice rose to its highest pitch. "Hear that?" he shouted. "That's my father. Look, he's an old man. Hasn't flown in years. And he's got my boy up there with him. I want help when he tries to land. Get that? HELP!"

He slammed down the phone and glared at Cornwall.

Cornwall strolled to the kitchen door. "Might as well watch the show," he said cheerfully. "Now that you've put this into the Chief's hands, there'll be plenty to look at. Nothing that man loves more than a *case.*"

In town, Gertie parked her old car in front of the tiny post office. She gathered up the letters she had ready to mail and stepped out on the sidewalk.

"Hi, there, Gertie," Ben, the Postmaster, called out from the doorway. He jiggled a large box he was carrying. "You're just in time. Do me a favor, will you, and mind the store while I run across the street and put these ladybugs into the Chief's car?"

"What on earth is he going to use ladybugs for?" Gertie asked. "Adding members to the police force, I suppose."

Ben grinned. "Nope. His wife believes in organic gardening, and these things eat aphids, or something."

Just as Ben placed the ladybugs on the back seat of the prowl car, the Chief came storming out the door of his office, shouting back at someone inside, "Notify the Highway Patrol. And call the hospital for an ambulance. Better phone the airport and the FAA office while you're at it."

Ben stepped up. "Say, Chief, I—"

"No time now, Ben. Got an emergency here."

As he whirled off in the prowl car, the many-colored little plane droned gaily high above Main Street. "Ragwing!" Gertie exclaimed in delight. "Three's getting his ride."

Ben crossed the street. "Looks like he—HEY! Look at that!"

A state motorcycle trooper thundered along Main Street, hot on the Chief's trail.

"You mean *hear* that!" Gertie exclaimed, covering her hearing aid. "You don't suppose he's out to nab the Chief for speeding, do you?"

Ben frowned. "Nope—not from what I heard the Chief yelling a minute ago. He was ordering out the Highway Patrol and an ambulance and the FAA. Say, I get those initials mixed up. Federal Agriculture Association, do you think? Maybe Abner's crop-dusting license expired."

Gertie gasped. "Do you mean to say that man called the FAA? Why, that's the Federal Aeronautics Authority. Sakes! Abner's only taking the boy up for a joy ride. Looks as though the Government is poking its nose into everything these days. I'm getting myself out to Abner's. Looks to me like he's going to need a few *friends*."

She ran to her ancient car. "Come on, Ben. Hop in."

Ben took a step forward, then stopped. "Can't, Gertie," he said sadly. "The mail's gotta go through."

"See you later, then," Gertie cried. Waving a swift goodbye she went galloping out of sight along Main Street.

Hardly had she gone when a second motorcycle shot through town. It was too much for Ben. He slammed the post office door, locked it, and leaped into his red, white and blue mail truck. "Heck!" he exclaimed aloud. "The mail's gotta go through, but it can go through backwards this time. I'll make deliveries on the way home from Abner's. Gertie's right. Abner's going to need all the friends he can get."

But it was Grimes at the airport who needed friends—or at least someone willing to speak to him. He hung on to his mike. "Ragwing! Come in Ragwing! Airport to Ragwing! Come in Ragwing."

His hands tightened on the mike. "Abner Therman! Come IN. What's the matter with you? You deaf?"

CHAPTER 11

Grimes wasn't the only one left with no one to talk to. Cornwall also had run out of people. High above him, Abner and Three merrily circled the sky. And down the lane, Two, still dressed in pajamas and robe, was scooting the farm truck toward the highway.

"Hey! Wait for me!" Cornwall shouted, running hard behind the truck. But Two kept going.

Cornwall disgusted, puffed to a stop. He turned and jogged back up the drive. "Knew it all along," he muttered. "A man's best friend is his horse."

Far above the excitement on the ground, Abner and Three swept and swooped above trees, fields and rooftops.

"Guess we've seen all the sights," Abner shouted back.

"Couldn't we just keep flying around?" Three yelled.

"Sure. No need to land right away. We can just sit up here shouting nice as you please."

Three grinned. "What would you like to shout about? The Red Baron?"

Abner took a deep breath. "Nope. Want to shout about your changing schools."

There was no reply from the rear cockpit, and after a pause, Abner went on. "I guess I really want to talk about change. You didn't want to

111

come here this summer, but I guess it's turning out better than you thought."

This time Three's shouted words came instantly. *"Is it! Sure is!"*

Abner smiled. "Well, there's change for you. Never know what's going to come of it. Me, for instance. Flying around like this—that's some change! Now, take your dad. He needs change, too. He needs a change from rushing around, living in hotels, not having a real home anywhere. He needs a house—a house with a boy in it."

There was a long wait. "What'd you think?" Abner finally shouted.

"Dad didn't say anything like that to me. How come you're asking that, Abner?"

This time the wait for an answer was in the front cockpit. Then Abner called loudly, "Well, I got it in mind I hope you stay in California. I guess I need you two Abners."

Three's shouted reply was serious. "I'll think about it."

"Settled! Now how about your learning to fly this plane—right now?"

Down on the highway a hitchhiker stood waiting along the empty stretch of road. Up went his thumb as a car approached in the distance. Down it went when he realized it was a police car.

The Chief roared by, not stopping to investigate the stranger. No sooner had the hitchhiker recovered from this happy surprise than two highway patrolmen roared by on motorcycles. As they zoomed off, Gertie's car came chugging into view. But she had her mind on other matters and never

glanced at the figure beside the road. "Looks like that old lady is trying to catch up with the Law," the hitchhiker muttered, staring up the road. "What's going on around here?"

A sudden, loud blast of a horn made him jump backward. This time it was a red, white and blue mail truck that was burning up the highway.

Up ahead, the hitchhiker could see that a second road must cross the main highway, because a white ambulance was speeding along it, siren going full blast. And right behind it another car held a fast pace—the FAA man racing to the scene. But what scene? The hitchhiker shrugged his shoulders and began walking, not even bothering to hold up his thumb as Abner Therman II, green-striped pajama sleeves blowing in the wind, went whizzing by.

Unseen by any of this strange traffic was Cornwall. In honor of the occasion, he had knotted a fresh, red bandanna about his neck, and put on his very best white Stetson—the one he never wore in the barn lest Ragwing fall on it. Free of fences, motorcycles, automobiles and people, he rode his under-exercised black horse across the purple sage. And the mighty stallion, mane flying, was clearly enjoying every minute of this unexpected return to the good old days of life on the range.

Neither Abner nor Three glimpsed the scene below. Something else was holding their attention—Ragwing's motor. The regular beat of the VW's 36 horsepower was breaking. The engine coughed, stopped, gulped, started—and stopped.

Three forgot all about Wakefield Academy, or the Red Baron, either. And Abner suddenly for-

got about the past or the future. This was NOW
—and they both knew it.

Abner's voice reached Three as though from a
cloud. "We're going to have to take her down,
Son."

"You mean we—we crash-land?"

"Nothing that serious," Abner shouted. "Just
the carburetor acting up. Half a minute on the
ground with a screwdriver will fix it." Then he
added, "If I can find a place to light."

Cornwall looked up as he heard Ragwing's motor pop, splutter like a string of damp firecrack-
ers, then die. "Oh, oh!" He dug his heels into his
horse's flanks and changed direction. With luck, he
and Ragwing would show up at the same place at
the same time. But the little plane was losing altitude fast.

"If he can just bring her down smooth on the
highway," Cornwall prayed.

Above him, Abner fought for every foot of altitude. Three leaned forward, red banderole stream-
ing in the wind. "You concentrate on the controls,
Abner. I'll go on lookout," he said in a steady
voice. "Hey! the highway's ahead."

Abner glanced downward. "We'll just make it."

"Can you land her all right?" Three asked, trying to keep the tremble out of his voice.

"Land all right!" Abner chuckled. "It's a road,
isn't it? Say! I remember one time in the city, I
landed on the roof of a big department store. Tax-
ied all the way from ladies-ready-to-wear to the
complaint department." He looked over the side
again. "Look down at that crossroad!" he exclaimed.

Three gazed down. Cars seemed to be coming from everywhere, and scrambling in a kind of traffic jam at the intersection. "What are they doing?" he shouted in dismay.

"Ganging up on us," Abner said grimly, wasting no words.

Down below it looked as though the traffic was trying to sort itself out and chase Ragwing. "If we land here," Three shouted, "they'll stop us from flying again, won't they?"

"Never took a crate up yet without bringing her home," Abner shouted cheerfully. "Too late to start now."

Already Ragwing was skimming the highway traffic. "Listen, Three," Abner called, "we'll make her yet. You take hold of that crop-dusting lever I told you about. And do exactly as I tell you."

Three grabbed the lever. Struts whining, Ragwing passed over the line of pursuing vehicles. They all speeded up to follow. Beyond the crossing, Ragwing's wheels skimmed the pavement.

"DUST!" Abner shouted.

Three pulled back on the lever. "Powder River! Let her buck!"

Dust. It was everywhere—a blinding, curling yellow cloud billowing from the tail of the little biplane.

Up and down the highway, brakes squealed, and vehicles came to a stop.

In the prowl car, the box of ladybugs lurched forward and smashed. But the Chief was so busy winding up the car windows he didn't even hear the bumping sound the box made as it crashed to the floor. "That Abner!" he yelled aloud. Those words were his last for some time. Ladybugs by the hundreds rushed for freedom. They flew into each other. They flew into the Chief. And to the mad wailing of sirens and honking of horns, made their escape out the door with the frantic, leaping Chief of Police.

Screened from view by the dust cloud, Ragwing quivered to a stop and Abner stood up in the cockpit, screwdriver in hand. "Be done in a jiff, Son. Stay where you are."

"Hey! Abner. *Look!*" Three yelled in excitement.

Abner turned in time to see Cornwall come up at a fast gallop from the nearby field and pull his horse to a rearing stop.

"What are you supposed to be?" Abner cried out, startled not only by Cornwall's arrival but at his splendid appearance. "The Lone Ranger?"

Cornwall guided his horse to Ragwing's side. "Don't have time to argue, Flyboy. Gimme that screwdriver. Couldn't you hear her starvin' for fuel?"

He took the screwdriver from the startled Abner and hastily dismounted. "Now when I holler, you give her a little throttle. Understand?"

"Sure I understand," Abner said. "And I hope you do, Cowboy." Anxiously, he looked back over his shoulder. "Here they come. Hurry it up."

Three shouted in excitement. "Look at that man in pajamas. He's running ahead of everybody. *Why, it's Dad!*"

"Hurry up, Cornwall," Abner begged.

"Don't rush me," Cornwall yelled back. He stepped away from the engine. "That does 'er, Abner. She's fixed."

Before Two could reach Ragwing's tail, the little plane began to move. "Dad! Three! Wait!" he shouted.

The roar of the engine drowned the rest of his words, and the slipstream nearly whipped his bathrobe off and flapped in Miss Gertie's face.

The group that followed behind her ducked.

"Come on," Two yelled at the motorcycle troopers. "They may need our help!"

"Not as much as we do," growled one of the men. But they leaped on their machines to rush ahead and block off Ragwing before she could lift into the air once more.

Too late. Each trooper swerved off the highway as Ragwing came swooping up.

"Why didn't *you* stop them, Cornwall?" Two shouted angrily. "They could both be killed!"

Cornwall looked over at the tangle of cars in the settling dust. He yawned lazily. " 'Pears to me it's safer in the sky than down here on the road."

"But what's my father hope to gain by this?" Two asked, his voice shaking.

Cornwall looked him square in the eye. "Nothin'. Pass a little history on to the boy. Do somethin' together—for the last time."

Two didn't speak for a moment. "Then what?" he asked.

"Fly back to the farm."

"You sure?"

"That's what he told me," Cornwall replied, mounting his horse.

Two turned to the group. "Back to the cars. They're heading for the farm."

While the traffic jam untangled, Abner and

Three were once more each looking delighted as Ragwing purred along.

"Jets fly too high, just like I said," Abner called back.

"Can't see enough up so high," Three agreed loudly.

They could certainly see enough from Ragwing. Fields, woods, streams, and—a reception committee gathering along either side of the farmhouse driveway.

"Dear me," Abner said mildly.

"What?"

"Trouble downstairs."

Three peered downward. "Oh, Do we *have* to go down?"

"Not afraid, are you?"

For a second. Three touched the wings on his pocket. "Nope. Just that I want to stay up here with you and Ragwing and fly and fly."

"Wish we could, Three, but we're running out of gas."

There was silence behind him. Then Three leaned forward. "Abner—you—you're not going to get into trouble, are you? I mean, trouble about taking me up and all that?"

"Hope so," Abner shouted cheerfully. "at my age there's not much trouble left for a fellow to get into. Wouldn't want to waste any chances." His hand tightened on the stick. "Ready?"

"Ready."

Ragwing began her dive.

CHAPTER 12

Everyone in the farmhouse yard stared skyward as Ragwing made her down swoop.

Gertie, Ben and Abner II were in one group—faces tense, fingers crossed.

In another cluster near the ambulance were the two highway patrolmen, the FAA man, and the Chief, all looking fearful for the safety of Abner and Three.

Ragwing made a perfect three-point landing, skimmed the highway, and slowed for her turn up the drive.

It was the Chief who broke the tension of the onlookers. Still decked out with ladybugs, he began swatting his arm about. "All right, now," he yelled at one last ladybug. "You git. Git! GIT." Then in an even louder voice, he added, "Fly away home. And that's an ORDER!"

A cheer went up from Abner's friends as Ragwing came to a stop, and Abner and Three stood up. But the officials, including the Chief, stared sternly at the flyers.

As Three climbed down from the cockpit, his father ran forward. He flung his arms around Three and hugged him tight. Three hugged back. Nothing like it had ever been seen at Wakefield Academy.

Abner's arrival safe on earth was spectacular. Gertie threw herself around his leather jacket and kissed him loudly, while Postmaster Ben managed to grab at least one hand and pump it up and down heartily, "That's the way to go, Abner. That's the way to go!"

Abner grinned. "Hold it Ben. I haven't gone yet." He looked over Gertie's shoulder. "Oh, oh! Four bandits at twelve o'clock high!" He stepped forward to the group of officials.

"Mr. Therman," the FAA man said sternly. "I'm from the regional FAA office, and I'm going to have to impound that airplane."

The Chief was not to be outdone by any outsider. He stepped up. "And what's this I hear about a stolen motor, Abner?"

Abner looked at him coolly. "You got some ladybugs on you there, Chief. Supposed to bring you good luck."

Two stepped in front of the Chief. "It was *my* motor. And he didn't steal it. He borrowed it."

The FAA man brushed everyone out of the way, and began instructing the troopers to move Ragwing into the barn. He turned to Abner. "Once I put my seal on that aircraft, it's not to be moved. Is that understood?"

Two tightened the cord of his bathrobe and spoke in a dignified, chilly voice. "Will it be okay if I take my motor back?"

"It's a great little power plant," his father said.

The FAA man frowned. "Oh, I suppose so," he said crossly. "But this is very irregular. Very! I don't know where to start with you, Therman. I can't even begin to count the rules and regulations you've broken. No inspection of reconstructed aircraft. No final registration. No radio communication. Whole flight illegal." He paused. "I'm sorry,

but I'm going to have to take your pilot's license."

Abner searched the pockets of his leather jacket, without success.

The FAA man's jaw dropped. "You do *have* a license, don't you?"

Abner Two spoke hastily. "License or not, did you ever see a better job of flying?"

And Gertie said angrily, "It's getting so the Government has its nose in everything."

Postmaster Ben turned pink. "That's the second time I've heard you say that, Gertrude. And as a public servant, I resent it."

The FAA man spoke impatiently. "The license. *Please!*"

"Ah! Here we are," Abner said calmly, pulling a flat oilskin-wrapped paper from his pocket. He carefully removed the card it contained and handed it over to the FAA man.

For a moment, Gertie was half-afraid that at least one person representing the Government wouldn't live to *get* his nose into anything—ever again. The poor man's eyes had a glassy stare, and his face had gone pale.

"Anything wrong?" Abner Two asked, and Three looked up anxiously at his grandfather.

Speechlessly the FAA man handed over the license.

"Looks okay to me," Two said coolly, handing it back. "It's signed ORVILLE WRIGHT."

"Is this real?"

"Sure is," Three spoke up. "Abner went to Kitty Hawk."

"Did Orville Wright teach you to fly?" the FAA man almost gasped.

Abner nodded calmly. "Uh-huh. Nice man. Knew his onions."

The FAA man's voice turned respectful. "I—I don't know. This is a historical document. Valuable personal property. No rules for this one."

The Chief's face turned raging red. "You're not going to let him off, are you? Why—"

"I didn't say that!" the FAA man exclaimed sharply. "It's simply that I'm taking the whole case under advisement."

At that moment, there was a sound of pounding hooves, and everybody turned to see Cornwall come galloping up the driveway, pull up, leap gracefully from his black steed, and loop the reins handily over the porch railing.

He turned to the crowd. "You folks want some coffee? Y'all look like you got up before breakfast." He smiled at Gertie. "You, too, Gertie. Time you tasted a real cup of Java."

"Sorry, Cornwall," Gertie replied coldly. "I failed to have my hearing aid turned up. Would you repeat that please?"

Cornwall's smile faded, "Java," he shouted.

"Oh, *coffee!*" Gertie smiled again. "And perhaps you'll give us some of those delicious hard biscuits you make." She turned to the others. "And just *maybe* he'll let us see the cement mixer he uses. Shall we all go inside?" Grinning, she led the way.

Three and Abner watched the others go up the steps, then both looked toward the open barn doors where the morning sun managed to catch Ragwing's cheery tail rudder.

"I'll *never* forget today. Never, Grandpa," Three said half-shyly.

"Grandpa?" Abner looked down. "Well, well. I kind of like the sound of that. Good word."

"It was different before," Three began. "But now—well now us Californians got to stick together."

Abner grinned. "You'd better go have that talk with your dad."

"Aren't you coming in?" Three asked Abner.

"In a minute, Son. You go ahead."

Three found his father in the bedroom, changing into daytime clothes. "Say, Dad," he began, leaning against the bedpost. "What would you think of me going back to San Francisco with you? I mean, sort of for *good* I mean—for *us* to live there?"

"For good?" Two asked.

Three nodded. "Except, of course, when we come down here to visit Grandpa."

Two grinned. "It's a deal!"

Three whirled away. "Wait 'til I tell Grandpa. Will he be surprised!"

"Wait a minute, Three. I forgot something. Here's a letter for you. Came to me marked PLEASE FORWARD."

Abner hurriedly wiped a sleeve across misty eyes as he heard footsteps pounding toward the barn. Saying goodbye to Ragwing was something he hadn't wanted to share—even with his co-pilot.

"Abner! Grandpa! Abner!" Three yelled as he came flying into the barn. "Here's something you're NEVER going to believe." He waved his letter excitedly.

"A letter from your girl back East!" Abner exclaimed.

Three looked sharply up at his grandfather.

"You've been watching cowboy shows on Miss Gertie's TV," he said sternly.

"Well, you told me it was something I'd never believe," Abner chuckled.

"Well, just listen to this!" Three began to read.

Dear Three:
Got your dad's address from Captain Willoughby. I have to tell you we can't be roommates after all. I'm moving out West with my mother and her new husband. His name is Jim and is okay. He took me to an airshow. Wish you'd had a chance like that. Nothing much to write about. Was thinking about your name. Why don't you call yourself Ab? That way you won't have to keep on explaining about one, two, three, and even *four*.

Yours truly,
Billy Norton

P.S. We're moving to San Francisco—about as far from Wakefield as you could get, I guess. Write me and I'll write you my new address when I get one. Better luck with airshows next summer. Meantime, Hay Hay! Farmer!

Three looked up. " 'Better luck with airshows next summer.' Wait 'til I write him I was IN one *this* summer!"

Three's grandfather grinned. "Say, how're you going to sign your letter to Billy?"

Three looked thoughtful. "Well," he said slowly, "now that you're 'Grandpa,' I think I'll just go ahead and sign it 'Abner,' that is—if it's okay with you."

Abner Therman grinned. "You bet it's okay!"

"I cannot believe you talked me into this," Dionne said.

She speared a piece of lame-looking chicken with the cheap airline fork and watched the grease drip off it.

"Look, I'm sorry," I said. "I know you can't order the diet meal without twenty-four hours' notice, but Tai needs us *now.*"

De made a face. "I can't believe you talked me into going to New York at all."

"But what about Tai?" I said. "De, we're her t.b.'s. If she can't count on us, who can she count on?"

Dionne shrugged. "But, Cher—New York City. Two innocent girls from sunnier climes—aren't you scared?"

I tried to focus on the positive. I mean, being from California and all. "De—New York City, fashion capital of the world. Home of Donna Karan, Ralph Lauren, CK."

"You think they live in Brooklyn with Tai?" Dionne asked.

**Don't miss out on any of Cher's
furiously wicked adventures!**

CLUELESS
A novel by H. B. Gilmour
Based on the film written and directed by
Amy Heckerling

CLUELESS™: CHER'S GUIDE TO . . . WHATEVER
By H. B. Gilmour

CLUELESS™: CHER NEGOTIATES NEW YORK
A novel by Jennifer Baker

and look for:

CLUELESS™: AN AMERICAN BETTY IN PARIS
A novel by Randi Reisfeld
(Coming mid-January 1996)

and

CLUELESS™: ACHIEVING PERSONAL PERFECTION
A novel by H. B. Gilmour
(Coming mid-March 1996)

Archway Paperbacks
Published by POCKET BOOKS

Cher Negotiates New York

A Novel by Jennifer Baker

AN ARCHWAY PAPERBACK
Published by POCKET BOOKS
New York London Toronto Sydney Tokyo Singapore

AN ARCHWAY PAPERBACK *Original*

An Archway Paperback published by
POCKET BOOKS, a division of Simon & Schuster Inc.
1230 Avenue of the Americas, New York, NY 10020

™ and copyright © 1995 by Paramount Pictures

ISBN: 0-671-56868-X

First Archway Paperback printing December 1995

10 9 8 7 6 5 4 3 2 1

AN ARCHWAY PAPERBACK and colophon are
registered trademarks of Simon & Schuster Inc.

Printed in the U.S.A.

IL:7+

Cher Negotiates
New York

Chapter 1

It was like this total Coke commercial moment. You know—a crowd of majorly attractive guys and gals, everyone having fun and oozing sex appeal, a choice tune pumping out of monster speakers. It was a club everyone wanted to be part of.

Josh took my hand and led me through the room of partiers, out onto the patio. In the velvet moonless sky, a few stars shone almost brightly enough to compete with the ones who made their home down here in Beverly Hills.

"Having fun, Cher?" Josh asked, pulling me close. If my allergies hadn't been acting up, I would have been able to smell the sweet-spicy combo of his shampoo and aftershave. You know—that whole romance novel kind of deal. Actually, it was still kind of new to me. I was always really good at taking care of everyone else's love life. Like these two teachers, Mr. Hall and Miss Geist. Well, actually, they were Mr. and Mrs. Geist-Hall now, and they were just exactly like two teenagers, except with less hair and more liver spots. But that's another story.

Anyway, for the longest time I was sort of like the Dear Abby of Beverly Hills High, except that when it came to myself, I was clueless. I'd been waiting around for The One, and he'd been right under my nose without my even suspecting.

See, Josh's mother and my father had been married for a little while a few years back, so we'd even lived under the same roof and everything. Josh was always pretending he was the big brother—always wanting what was best for me. But really he was like this scrawny bird-and-bug kind of nature nerd. He'd been on a mission to get José, our gardener, to turn the back lawn into some kind of refuge for the animal kingdom. Plant a forest, dig a frog pond, make like some Club Med paradise for the lower species. So that when I was trying to catch some rays by the pool, there might be reptiles and stuff dropping by. Ugh. Enough to make you want to go right out and buy a genuine snakeskin belt, instead of the do-right faux kind I wore.

And, of course, then I was so used to thinking of Josh as this loser that it had taken me way too long to notice he'd turned into this major Baldwin. And a nice guy—a rarity for Baldwins. Plus, he was even a college guy now, too. I mean, sure, there are a few total babes at my school—great bods in their 501s—but I was looking for something more . . . evolved, you know?

Anyway, Josh gave me a long slow kiss, and I actually shivered. And not because of my backless Calvin Klein shift. I could get used to this boyfriend thing.

"Mmm, thanks for being here," I murmured between more kisses. Josh had to be pretty stoked on me to be spending the night at a high school party.

"Hey, this isn't too rough," he whispered back, kissing me again.

The party was totally happening all around us. Over Josh's broad shoulder, I could see my best friend, Dionne, fighting with her boyfriend, Murray, down at the tennis court. They always seemed to choose the ideal spot to display the noisy side of their relationship. The court was lit up like a stage, and a crowd was gathering. De was lobbing Jell-O shots at Murray—forty–love, set point. And her white Anna Sui skirt that showed off her long dark legs was a winner, too. Her tennis instructor would have been proud.

"Woman, you best learn to show some respect for your man," I could hear Murray shouting, as a gelatinous blob hit him square in the face. A courtside roar went up. I knew he and De were loving the attention. Those two would succeed at becoming a tabloid Hollywood couple yet.

My other best friend, Tai, was somewhere inside,

dancing with her boyfriend, Travis. Tai was a new woman since she'd moved to Beverly Hills. She'd gone from New York City gutter rat to big-time Betty—with a little coaching from me and De and a big-time makeover from the outside in. And Travis, well, I could picture that way he had of kind of rocking forward and back, with his mouth hanging open, a holdover from his crispier days. But since he'd cleaned up his act, step by step by all twelve steps, he was really pretty righteous. Even if his dancing was stuck in burnout mode.

Suddenly I realized that Josh was all like, "Come in, Cher. Where are you?"

"Oh. Sorry. I was just thinking how everything's so totally excellent. . . . That this is like the perfect night, you know?" Josh gave me a soft romantic kiss on the curve of my neck. "I mean, Paul Devere didn't even hurl in the pool tonight."

"And here I was thinking that maybe it was perfect because, well, like you and me . . ." Josh said lightly. "Besides, I think that Paul guy broke some priceless antique vase in the den."

"Oh, Josh, there are tons of those in Beverly Hills. And anyway, it *is* perfect because of you and me." I couldn't believe the gushy words coming out of my mouth. What was more amazing, I meant them. I was majorly, radically in love with Josh.

Right that second I couldn't have asked for anything more. Well, maybe my driver's license. But even failing my road test had a plus side to it. I'd convinced Daddy that I deserved an increase on my credit-card limit because my Jeep was just sitting in the garage unused. No gas bills, no upkeep, no insurance. And Daddy had agreed to fork over a percentage of what I was saving him.

It really doesn't get any better when you're sixteen.

Every light was on at Tai's. We could see her mother pacing around the living room of their trim brick house. We sat in Josh's red Spider, me and him in the front, Tai and Travis squished romantically in the back. Dionne and Murray were caravaning behind us in Murray's Jeep, a rap tune turned up so loud that we were all pulsing away to it, too, in our own car. As they pulled in behind us, one of them turned it down to a dull roar, so as not to alarm Mrs. Frazer.

"Aw, man, she's like wearing a path in the wall-to-wall," Tai moaned, her New York accent slightly softened by good California living. "And I just helped her pick it out new at the Rug Barn."

I winced at Tai's downscale shopping habits. There was only so far that her makeover could go.

Mrs. Frazer was doing major-league laps around the living room. "Wow, she's got to be like burning more calories than with *Buns of Steel*," I said.

"Yeah, she's pissed." Travis sort of giggled. "Trouble ahead, trouble behind . . ."

"Travis, shut up," Tai said. She sounded desperate. "You guys don't get it. She's gonna kill me."

I glanced at my museum-edition Movado. "Relax.

It's only five to one. We've barely gone over the dateline."

"She said for me to be home by midnight. Like I'm gonna turn into a punkin or something."

"Pumpkin. Way strict," I commented.

"She's been getting worse and worse ever since we moved here," Tai said. "Like when she was total toast in New York, I could do anything I wanted. But now that she's cleaned up her act, she's all Cindy Walsh and stuff."

"Who?" Josh wanted to know.

"Forget it, Josh," I said. Josh is like way too intellectual for *90210*. Except when he thinks no one's looking. "Too bad you can't send your mother off to Hong Kong, like the Walshes," I told Tai. "About time Brandon stops living with his mommy and daddy. I mean, Jason and Luke and everyone are practically fossils already. Who do they think they're fooling?"

"I don't know. Brandon's still a Baldwin," Tai said loyally. "Ay, did you know that Amber saw him eating lunch in some restaurant near Rodeo?"

"As if. Ambular's probably lying," I said. "Who was he with?"

"Are we going to sit here and gossip about some guy on TV?" Josh said.

Tai sighed. "Anything's better than going inside. I don't know. Maybe it's like too much for my mom. Taking care of me by herself, working two jobs, being all responsible, and stuff. She's such a mom now."

"She just needs a boyfriend," I said, reaching over and squeezing Josh's hand.

"Or two or three," Tai agreed. "I swear, she's never gonna let me out of the house again. Hey, listen. I got a great idea. How about we make a night of it. Like, if this is the last time I get to go out . . ."

"Daddy's going to go ballistic," I said, "but it has been a way special night so far. . . . Yeah, I'm totally there."

"Par-ty!" Travis put in.

I looked at Josh. "Cool," he said. "How about switching gears and hitting campus. I could go for some tunes and some java at Drink Me, if we're going to do a late-nighter."

Drink Me was the grunge-infested coffeehouse at Josh's college. Everyone was some budding angst-ridden artiste or some neo-hippie philosopher. But Josh had come along to the Beverly High party, so I shrugged. "Whatever."

"Whoa, college bound!" Travis cackled. "And I only failed my PSATs twice already."

We pulled a U-ie, and Josh called to Dionne and Murray. "Follow us, okay?"

I thought I saw Tai's mother open a window and stick her head out at about the same time Murray and De cranked up the hip-hop. But by that time we were peeling away down the road like dead skin off a sunburn.

Chapter 2

Drink Me was like your basic rec room meets "Unplugged." I figure every college has one. Tiny stage with a single white spotlight. A neo-hippie-style Betty with a kind of nice, kind of flat voice coming through the crackly mike. Low ceilings, a few bare bulbs—some red, some yellow, some burnt out—and lots of smoke.

That meant lots of smokers. College smokers. The kind who would hit the streets babbling about Green Peace and clean air during the day, then come nightfall you'd find them huddled together in little hideaways polluting the planet, not to mention their not-yet twenty-year-old lungs. Okay, so some of them had hit the big two-oh, but they were still weird.

The clothes were way last Tuesday. It was mostly

flannel with a hint of chamois. I swear, some of the kids had just added a few grimy patches to the same pair of ripped-at-the-knees jeans that had gotten them through four years of high school. It was like the major transition from grunge to slacker. What-ever.

Needless to say, De, Tai, and I didn't quite fit in. De tried wiping down a little of her makeup, and Tai untucked her shirt from her pants. It was about as close as she could get to her old New York hippie self, but she was wearing designer silk, so she wasn't about to fool too many people. I was backless and skimpy to begin with, and there was no way I was going to put a grunge slit in my Calvin. Besides, I figured a lot of the stares I was receiving were because I looked way decent.

We grabbed an empty table in the back, and Josh and Murray went up to the little front counter to score double mochaccinos for all.

"Just think, Cher," Josh said, when he got back and sat down with the javas. He gave me a little squeeze. "In a few years, this could be you."

All of a sudden the idea of earning a college degree through correspondence classes in the safety of my own multimillion-dollar Beverly Hills mansion was flashing through my head.

Josh laid a soft kiss on my neck. "I know just what you're thinking, Cher." He gave me a look that I took for one hundred percent serious, then leaned in and smothered me with another wet one. "Don't ever change a bit. Really."

I was all melt, melt, gush, gush. All of a sudden it didn't matter where I was. College, high school, stuck in traffic on the Santa Monica Freeway—as long as I was with my honey, everything was way excellent.

The rest of the world disappeared for a moment as I let myself get gobbled up in Joshdom. All of a sudden, a monster blast of feedback split the air. The pretty girl on stage tapped her finger on the mike. She ran her fingers through her wavy dark hair and gave a little toss of her head. "Test, test, okay cool," she said. "Just needs a little more treble."

Josh looked toward the stage. "She's pretty good. She's in a class of mine. I always thought she was smart, but I never knew she could play so well."

Whatever.

The girl strummed a major chord and leaned in to the mike. "I think my last song is something we can all relate to. It's called 'Mental, Mental, Existential.' I wrote it—well, actually it sort of wrote itself. Descartes, Kant, Nietzsche. I mean, they're intense enough one at a time, but when it's four A.M. and you're cramming for a midterm and these dead old wise men are coming at you faster than you can think—"

She strummed a few more chords as she got ready to sing. I noticed this I-know-exactly-where-you're-at kind of grin on Josh's face. It sort of bugged me because, when it came to existentialism and most other isms, I was as clueless as the next person.

"Anyway, what can I say?" the girl continued. "This song might touch something deeper if you all close your eyes and get into your own personal space for a little while. 'Mental, Mental, Existential,' it's an existential thing." She strummed a few more of the same chords and started singing. " 'Hey, I was alone. Hey, I am alone. Hey, I am alone. Hey—hey, hey . . .' "

I looked around the room, and sure enough, it was lids shut. Josh had given himself over to the moment, too, and so had Travis and Tai, who seemed to be taking advantage of the chance to reexperience what deep space felt like.

It was just De and Murray and I who remained wide-eyed in amazement. We did our own version of existence, wrapping arms around each other and pulling close for a whisper fest.

Murray started with a little tune of his own. "Dig the scene, jelly bean. This college thang's flippin', if you know what I mean."

"College. This is college!" I whispered, trying hard not to ruin the big "moment" for everybody. I tried to imagine our high school crowd in a situation like this. My dear sweet capital-F Friend, Christian? He might pretend to shut his baby blues, but he'd keep one open just a little to check out the cute boys— that's the way he went. And he'd keep the other one open slightly to check out who was checking him out.

It was impossible to picture any of our crowd submitting to this existential shut-eye thing. Not us. We always had to stay way on top of things. In our world it was all, you snooze you lose. One slip-up and your boyfriend would get snatched up. Whatever.

Like a few months ago, Taj blinked and she lost Elton to Amber. Not that it mattered, because Elton proved himself to be one slimy, slippery eel—just perfect for Ambular the chameleon. Elton sort of became an ex-pal one night after a party in the Valley when he offered me a ride home and then tried to force his teendom on me. In the end, he left me stranded in some creepy alley—just me, my Alaïa, a mugger, and a gun. Remembering that one was enough to keep my eyes open forever!

" 'Mental, Mental, Existential. Mental, Mental, Existential. It's an existential thing . . .' " She wailed the refrain, adding reverb and feedback in just the right—philosophical—places.

Surely her song was going to end soon? Not so fast. Every time she mentioned that Nietzsche dude or some other ancient sage, a couple of shut-eyed intellectuals in the crowd would stroke their fuzzball goatees and nod in agreement. Josh was one of them, and it was beginning to bug me more than I wanted it to. Then again, fuzzball and all, he was a major Baldwin. Pitter, patter—I zeroed in and surprised him with a wet one on the nose. But it was, like, "Hey, high school girl, can't you see I'm thinking."

Was I missing something? So I tried—I really tried—to shut my eyes and see what this existential thing was all about. The first thing that popped into my head was makeup. I wondered if you were all alone in a forest and your eyeliner was on crooked, would it really look so bad?

"Hey," I heard De whispering to Murray. "You think Cher's evolving?"

That did it. I bit down hard to keep from howling, and my eyes were opened for the remainder of the night.

" 'Mental. Mental. Existential. Mental. Mental—' " She took a long pause, played two heavy chords, and finished. " 'It's an existential thing . . . All right!' "

Chronic applause. As for De, Murray, and me, we just thought it was excellent that it was over.

Tai's and Travis's eyes stayed closed. They'd fallen happily asleep in each other's loving arms. Tai, the New York street urchin transformed into a serious Betty, and Travis, skateboard-slacker-waste product, step-by-stepping his way to a full-on Evolvement. What can I say except they were, in Tai's words, "Umbuh-lievably cute."

That gave me the urge to grab my hottie for a smooch, despite the fact that he was still clapping for the cute, existential whiner. "You're still a major Baldwin," I told Josh, planting a kiss on his lips. "Even if you are a hopeless complaint-rocker."

Josh seemed a little annoyed. "There are a few of us left who take existence seriously, Cher. Believe it or not, there is merit in trying to transcend a world ruled by Calvin and Jordache."

"Jordache? As if!" Josh was clueless when it came to fashion, but I loved him anyway.

"Well, thank you, guys, for being such a great audience," said the girl on the stage. "And now I better go finish this paper I've got due." And then she was packing up her guitar and winding her way between tables and heading dead-on for us. With way too big a smile for *my* Josh.

"Hi, Josh," she said. Even her wave bothered me.

"Hi, Simone. You sounded great."

Simone? Like he actually knew her name already?

She smiled much too condescendingly at all of us high school kiddies. I gave Josh a not-so-little poke in the ribs—so he introduced me fast. I grabbed his arm just to let her know who belonged to who.

"Simone—like Nina Simone," I said. Well, I had to say something.

She gave a precious little smile. "Actually, my parents named me for Simone de Beauvoir."

Simone de who?

There was a way long pause. I looked at De for help, but she just shrugged, clueless like the rest of us.

Josh started in. "You know, the philosopher—"

"I knew that," I hurried. "Whatever."

There was another long uncomfortable pause, and then Josh and Simone were on to college things and we were left in kiddie-land.

Simone was showing off her aptitude for vocabulary. Five-, six-, and seven-syllable words that Webster himself would have had to look up. That many syllables from someone who only knew three chords on the guitar.

From lengthy words they segued into a rousing game of Name that Brain. That dude Nietzsche came up a few more times—he was starting to bug me out. And a whole list of others, people I figured I'd be learning about when I got to college. But I wasn't there yet, and I was starting to worry that Josh and I were planets apart.

When Nietzsche's name popped up again, I couldn't take it anymore. "So what's that paper on, See-moan?" I asked. "You know, the one you told everybody you had to finish up."

"Oh, that. Philosophy. It's about truth and beauty—"

Now, there's something I know a lot about. I hardly ever lie, and when it comes to beauty, I know a Betty when I see one.

"I'm doing it from a Kantian perspective," Simone added. "Although there'll be some of the more foundational stuff in there, too. You know, the primary sources," she said, matter-of-factly. "Plato, Descartes, a little Hume."

Josh seemed to be falling for it in a major way. It was like Simone had him nodding to her beat, whether his eyes were open or closed.

"Well, I guess you'd better go get to work," I said sweetly.

"Oh. Yeah," Simone said. "I'll see you around, Josh. I'm glad you kids made it to my show. See ya."

I hoped not.

Well, you can imagine my mood swing when the door closed after Simone and Josh put his arm around me. "Hope you guys weren't too bored by the college rap. Anyone for another round of coffees?" Then he laid a major kiss on me and headed for the counter.

Huh? Did I miss something in the translation? Here I was stoked for a put-up-your-dukes fest, my first serious marital squabble with my first serious Baldwin. I looked at De for an explanation, but she wasn't any help at all.

"What's up, girlfriend?" De asked.

"Wait a minute," I said. "Didn't you all just see what I saw? Didn't Miss Existential Playmate of the Month just make a major come-on to Josh?"

De shrugged and nodded toward Josh, who was making his way back to us. "Cher, you'd better enjoy what you got, 'cause that boy is radically in love with you."

The second time we hit Tai's, the lights were off. She breathed a mochaccino-flavored sigh of relief, sucked face with Travis for a while, and finally let herself out of the car to tiptoe inside.

I wasn't as lucky.

"Cher?" Daddy's voice thundered the second I stepped into our big neo-colonial. I'd taken my Susan Bennis/Warren Edwards off, but even barefoot, I somehow got caught. I think you get like this extra hearing gene or something when you become a parent. Plus, I could feel the eyes in the painting of my mother looking down on me from the wall. I felt ashamed. My mother died when I was a baby. A freak accident during routine liposuction. I like to think she would have been proud of how I turned out. And I knew, if she were alive, that she wouldn't have been any more pleased than Daddy, right now.

"Cher, get in here!" he yelled from his study.

I peeked my head in. He was nursing a glass of amber liquid. "Daddy?" I said timidly. "You know your doctor said you're not supposed to be drinking that . . ."

"Oh, but it's okay for my sixteen-year-old daughter to stay out until three o'clock in the morning and give me a heart attack?"

"Daddy, we were just out having coffee. Nothing to worry about."

"'We'? You and Josh?"

I grimaced. Ever since Josh and I had gotten together Josh had been trolling for a demotion from star stepson to the Evil Boyfriend. I knew it was getting bad when Daddy stopped bothering to try to talk him down from his high principles and seduce him into the more lucrative corporate side of the legal profession. Didn't Daddy care anymore?

"Daddy, it wasn't Josh's fault."

"Josh's fault, your fault. You are not going to come home this late anymore. Do you understand?"

I frowned. "You come home late lots of nights."

"Cher, I come home late because I work late. I'm slaving over briefs and papers at the office."

"Well, don't you think it's hard work being one of the most popular girls at school? I have a reputation to keep up. I have a social schedule to fulfill. Don't you want me to be on top of the heap?"

Daddy was speechless for a second. I could tell I'd scored a point, there. After all, he was the one who'd taught me the fine art of the argument, and he was one of the best.

"And what happened to that mobile phone you've always got glued to your ear? I tried calling you on it three times."

"Maybe the battery ran down," I said. Then again, maybe not. I'd shut the ringer off on the way to Drink Me for this very reason.

"Look, Cher. This is the third time this month you've come home late. The third. And I don't want it happening again. Now, you'd better behave like a little angel for a while, do you hear me? Or no deluxe suite at Snowbird this Christmas."

I was properly chastened. No deluxe suite? "But, Daddy, all the other rooms have this really bad fluorescent lighting in the bathrooms. Remember a couple years ago when business was down and we had to go economy? Every time I looked at myself in that hotel mirror, I looked all washed out, and my makeup came out way awful. Plus, I got that Santa-size Barney for a ski instructor. I mean, I thought they had some minimum looks requirements for those jobs where people have to interact with the public."

"They were private lessons," Daddy said.

"Whatever. The point is—"

"The point is that you're going to do what I say," Daddy growled.

Christmas vacation was an awesomely long way away, but I put on my best smile. What else could I do? "Okay, Daddy," I said sweetly. "Now how about some fresh wheat grass juice instead of that Scotch?"

"Cher, don't push me," Daddy warned.

I decided that there would be better times to watch Daddy's health. "Good night, Daddy," I said, and kissed his stubbly cheek. "I'm sorry I made you worry about me."

"Don't let it happen again," he said. But then he cracked a small smile. "Good night, princess."

Yes! The deluxe suite was in my future, after all.

Chapter 3

*H*ey, Amber, seen Tai, today?" I whispered while Mr. Hall scribbled on the board. Amber shook her big hair. "Then pass it down," I added. As I leaned toward her, I spotted her new, furry, and, I have to say, hideous after-ski boots. As if there was likely to be snow on the ground in perfectly sunny, sixty-eight-degree Beverly Hills. But they'd had a major dumping up in Tahoe the night before, and half the school was talking about heading there this weekend. The guys from the Persian Mafia, snickering in Farsi in the back of the room, were as good as in their loqued-out Beamers and speeding toward the slopes already.

So just to be *au moment,* Ambular had poured herself into some baby-blue ski pants and a matching sweater that followed every surgically enhanced curve. And then there were those boots. "By the way," I said to her. "The dogs on your feet need a serious trim."

"So, just because your boyfriend's too PC for real fur, you don't have to get all jealous on me." She stuck one of those long-haired dogs out into the aisle to admire it better.

"As if!" I snorted. Amber was such a cavewoman. But she did pass along my message. I watched her whisper to Summer. Summer looked at me, shrugged, and passed the message up to Christian.

Christian turned around in his seat. "Sale at Agnès B.?" he said out loud, too cool to whisper.

"Not Tai's style," I answered.

"Not even," Summer agreed.

"Too bad," Christian said. "They've got some brutally handsome threads. I got a couple of pairs of pants and a silk dinner jacket. And in the women's section, I saw this yellow linen pleated mini that would look radical on you, Cher."

"Yeah?" I made a mental note to get to Agnès B. before the goods got picked through. Christian was the ultimate word on the best shopping in town. Just about any town.

Mr. Hall turned back toward the class, and his gaze kind of floated around until he found where the talking was coming from. He looked at us. His mud-colored sweater was covered with chalk. "Did one of you have something to say about the new Eastern Europe?" he asked mildly. I noticed he'd drawn a map on the board. It looked sort of like one of those thousand-piece puzzles with no reference points. How were any of us going to learn that?

"Actually, Mr. Hall, we were talking about the pre-Christmas sales," Christian answered. "And whether anyone had seen Tai today."

"Oh. I see." Mr. Hall frowned. "Tai. Tai Frazer." Suddenly his face lit up. "She was such a lovely bridesmaid," he said dreamily. Tai and Dionne and I had been bridesmaids at Mr. Hall and Miss Geist's wedding.

I blew out a breath. I was glad Hall and Geist were happy, but it was impossible to ignore the fact that I'd learned more in Hall's class when he was a strict, lonely little, shiny-headed bowling pin of a bachelor.

"About Eastern Europe, Mr. Hall," I said. I wanted to help him get back to where he was supposed to be. "You know, I could eat caviar on toast every night and never get tired of it."

Mr. Hall's brow wrinkled. "Yes, Cher. Well, that *is* a big export product for some of the countries we're discussing, today."

Elton waved his hand around so hard I thought it might fly off his arm. "Mr. Hall? Mr. Hall?"

"Yes, Elton?"

"Um, can I leave class and look for her?" he asked.

"Look for whom, Elton?"

"Tai."

"Oh. Right. Tai. Ah, no Elton, I don't think that would be a very good idea," Mr. Hall said. At least he hadn't given up *all* his standards.

"Well, can I have the bathroom pass, then?" Elton asked.

"Yo, Eltie, baby, you've shot down to the little boys' room twice already this period," Jon Bernstein called out. "You having trouble controlling yourself?"

Everyone lost it.

"Class! All right, now, class!" Mr. Hall yelled. "No, Elton. You may not have the bathroom pass again. And tomorrow I suggest you relieve yourself before my class begins. And may I remind all of you that midsemester grades are coming up, soon?" The old Mr. Hall could still rally just enough in a time of crisis.

At the mention of grades, we all got quiet fast. Mr. Hall even got the subject back to Eastern Europe and managed to stay there until the bell.

As for Tai, she was missing in action for the rest of the day. Not even Travis knew where she was.

I was in shock. I stared at Tai's mountain of luggage. She was Audi. I mean for good. And with a mismatched set of tow-up ugly Samsonite knock-offs, to boot.

"What—were you really going to leave without even saying anything to us?" I asked. I was hurt and angry. De and I had arrived at Tai's straight from school. And just in time. A few hours later, and Tai would be flying back to New York City, her luggage a fattening meal in the belly of the plane.

Tai sat on her faded sofa and shrugged miserably. She had on a pair of ratty jeans, and she hadn't bothered to do her makeup. Her eyes were red, as if she'd been crying. She hadn't even left the long arm of my fashion tutelage yet, and she already looked worse. If I hadn't been so buggin', I would have been tempted to whip out my compact and start fixing her up.

"I knew it was gonna be too hard to say goodbye to you." Tai sniffled. "I mean, you guys are like the best friends I've ever had. I didn't know if I'd be able to go, like, if I saw you first."

"Then don't go," Dionne said. "Girlfriend, are you crazy or something? What could possibly send you back there? Don't you know that Beverly Hills is full of ex-New Yorkers who had to fight and claw their way west? This is the promised land, honey. You can't leave."

"Yeah, and when they first came here, there weren't even any decent bagels or lox," I added. "Ask my father."

"You guys don't understand," Tai said. "I don't want to go. But my mom—she just gets worse and worse. After the other night, she grounded me for like the rest of my life."

"So you'll stay in for a while," I said. "Rent some videos, catch up on your movie-watching."

"Without a VCR?" Tai said.

I tried not to look shocked. Did they let you live in Beverly Hills without the basic necessities? Weren't there provisions for people in need? But I didn't want Tai to feel hopeless.

"Okay, so you'll tube out. Get an extra dose of Jason Priestley." I even resisted the urge to inform her that he was so two years ago. "You can invite Travis over. Snuggle up in the blue glow of the television." Frankly, it sounded sort of romantic to me.

Tai looked even more unhappy. "Except Travis is illegal goods, too. Mom thinks he's the reason I'm staying out all night."

"Travis? Tscha!" De said, flipping her hair extensions with a sharp snap of her wrist. "He can barely stay up past midnight."

Tai got this bittersweet smile. "Yeah, wasn't he cute the way he fell asleep on my shoulder at the coffee bar?"

"Well, then, how can you leave him?" I demanded.

"Yeah, he was buggin' when he didn't know where you were, today," De said, jumping in.

"He was?" Tai's smile grew bigger and sappier.

"Big time," I answered. "He was cruising around from table to table in the lunchroom on his skateboard, asking everyone if they'd seen you. He was calling you his Mrs."

"Aw." Tai sighed. "What was he wearing?"

De and I traded a glance. "Would you believe a navy linen Armani suit and new suede boots?" I deadpanned.

Tai gave a raw laugh. "Nah. No way. He had on some baggy jeans and a T-shirt and his Airwalks. You guys crack me up. I'm gonna totally miss you."

"And Travis?" I asked.

Tai's face fell. "You really know how to make a girl hurt."

"Then don't go!" De and I both said.

"Your mom'll chill out after a while. They always do," De said.

Tai sank farther back into the sofa. "You don't understand. I think she's losing it. Like she's trying so hard to be a real mom and all that she's killing both of us. It's my fault. I'm like this burden to her . . ."

I knew De and I were losing our battle. No one said anything for a while.

"It won't be so bad," Tai finally said. "I'll be living with my aunt out in Brooklyn. She's got a house with a backyard and everything." I pictured our Tai in some random little house, soaking up the sun in a lawn chair from Bradlees. Life could be so unfair.

We heard a honk outside. "The car service to the airport," Tai said. She got up. "So you'll tell Travis for me, right?"

"Do we have a choice?" I asked. I couldn't believe that Tai was really going.

"Tell him I—I love him," Tai said, swallowing hard. "I never said that to a boy before."

I felt my eyes get moist. I couldn't help it. But it was okay. I had on my waterproof mascara. "Look,

Tai. At least let us come out to the airport with you,"
I said.

She got this grateful little smile. "Really?"

"Seriously really," I said.

Dionne cast a wary look at the mismatched
luggage, but then she nodded, too.

"You guys are t.b.," Tai said.

Chapter 4

*T*he porter at LAX was wigging at the sight of all that faux Samsonite. But Daddy had always taught me the value of placing a few bills in someone's hand, so I gave him a nice fat tip. I knew that the goodbye-Tai scene was going to be emotional enough without the bag boy going postal in the middle of it. Anyway, I dropped him a fin and that was that.

After we checked Tai in, we headed straight for the gift shops. I mean, we couldn't send her off without a few choice going-away presents. And she'd have to have a few things for her family and pals, too. It just wouldn't be right to send the girl back to New York empty-handed.

I'd been to LAX enough to know where the juice stuff was. We whizzed by the first group of money munchers hawking their Sharper Image gadgets. I really didn't think Tai needed a golf-score calculator slash stock ticker or a toilet seat for her nonexistent cat.

But we found a totally awesome souvenir shop in the international departures terminal that was so Hollywood it probably made tourists wish they hadn't spent the big bucks at Disney.

"Way hot machine!" De whistled in amazement as we stood in front of The Future Is Here Photo-Op booth. De read the text on the screen. " 'Select your favorite star, pose for the camera, and you'll be together forever.' "

It was a machine made for the nineties—virtual reality meets consumer rip-off. I knew we'd be dropping big bucks on this one. "This'll be perfect for souvenirs for your New York pals, Tai."

"Yah, but it's like ten bucks a pop," Tai said. "I don't know."

I put my arm around her. "Look, Tai. It's our treat, okay? We want to send you back to New York in style. Now, who should we get you to pose with?"

"You guys are too amazing. Man, am I going to miss you," Tai said as she scanned the list of stars. "Sinatra, I guess. Yeah, it's always been like my family's dream to meet Frankie. If I gave them a picture of me hanging with Ole Blue Eyes they'd be so proud of me. Especially my aunt Rita—she'll frame it and invite the whole neighborhood over for a party."

"How about doing one for your friends?" I asked.

Tai breathed a long heavy sigh. "Yeah, I guess." You could tell she was majorly worrying. It was like she'd decided to go back to New York but totally forgot to think about what she was in for. "Maybe I should bring something for Lenny."

I sort of remembered that name. I think he was this guy from Tai's past who she'd been happy to leave behind when she came out to Beverly Hills. Lenny was the good-friend type who was always trying to be more than just a friend.

Tai was scanning the screen of famous faces and finally stopped on a picture of Jerry Garcia. "I don't know if Lenny's finished with his vigil. This'll probably choke him up too much."

De and I exchanged looks. "Didn't the fat guy die ages ago?" I asked. "But go for it, Tai. You and Jerry will look great together." I'd always thought Tai's past was so yesterday. Now I was a little worried that it was more like last century.

I gave Tai a quick hair redo and recolored her eye makeup for a nostalgic look for her moment with Frankie—real 1950s baby-doll lounge queen. Then, against my better taste, I hippied her up for Jerry by grabbing some totally ancient love beads and a pair of peace-sign earrings from the store. Then De and I got Tai to do some awesome posing. It was like the Tai makeover had continued into the eleventh hour.

"Hey, you guys hang here. I'll be back in a sec." I left Tai and De to wait for the photos to develop and slipped out to buy a present for Tai. I wanted to find something meaningful, something she could remember me by.

I popped my head into a little boutique and saw a great CK straw hat. No, way too summer vacation for New York. I spotted a classy camel-colored Isaac Mizrahi dress that totally went with a thick hand-tooled leather belt. But that look was more me than Tai. With Tai you had to work hard just to get her out of her 501s and into a pair of Guess. Besides, I wanted to buy her something really special.

I found just the thing next door. Tai didn't know it yet, but she was about to go cellular. The perfect going-away present because, well, wouldn't it be the next best thing to being there? And Daddy would approve, too, because he owned gobs of stock in all the cellular companies. I felt good about my brainstorm of an idea.

The only problem was which color to get. White was too L.A. The taupe one was nice, but not Tai. Grape, raspberry, or lemon? I finally decided on basic black. Even though it wasn't exactly lively, I knew it was the only color in New York.

"There you are, girlfriend!" De said, when I got back to the souvenir store. While I was gone, De had managed to fill a bag with stuff for Tai. I peeked in and gave a nod of approval at De's choices. A *Pulp Fiction* lipstick holder and makeup mirror, and some choice makeup purchases to go along with it; a leopard print halter; and a soon to be classic piggy bank in the shape of an Evian bottle. For Tai's college fund. And that all-important *Buns of Steel* tape. Couldn't let her leave without it.

"She's boarding in five minutes," De said, pointing at her way-over-the-top Goofy and Pluto watch that clashed with everything in the world.

There was so much to say as we ran toward the departure gate. "Don't forget that your base always goes on first," I reminded Tai.

"Yeah, I know. I'll remember," Tai said.

It had taken De and me plenty of hard work to get Tai to this point, and I wasn't about to let that slip away, no matter where she was living.

"And remember to check the weather report before you make any final decisions about eye shade and blush. Remember, sun means warm, so play up the reds and yellows. Cloudy means cool—blues and browns."

"Got it," Tai promised.

"And don't get sucked back into that my-mama-ain't-around-so-there's-no-one-ironing-my-clothes look," De insisted. "You're a fine-looking woman, Tai, remember that."

When we got to the gate and saw that people had already started boarding, Tai froze in her tracks for a second. I wished hard that she'd change her mind right there. But I knew there was no way she'd back out now. The faux Samsonite was already cargo.

"You guys have been so excellent," she said, struggling to hold back tears. "You're really umbuh-lievable. I know I'll never, ever find replacements for either of you."

"We'll always take you back, girl," De said, wiping away a few tears of her own. "I'm serious."

"We're your t.b.'s, Tai," I said. "You know there'll always be a place for you in Beverly Hills."

Tai shook her head as she lost her battle not to cry. "I wish this wasn't happening. But it's just the way it is, okay? I mean, it'll be great with my aunt and uncle in Brooklyn. Sure, it'll be groovy." But she was hardly convincing.

I pulled the phone out of my bag and handed it to Tai. "I got you a little something to keep you close. I already arranged to put the bill on my plastic, so go wild. As long as you call us."

Tai's mouth hung open. "Wow, my very first cellular. You're, like, so incredible. I can't believe how much I'm gonna miss you guys."

"Just call us a lot, okay," I said, biting down hard on my lip so that I wouldn't crack like the other two. "And remember, third-period algebra is the best time to get me."

We all huddled tight for a tear-jerker group hug. Wow, it was like a major phase of my life was getting all bent out of shape.

We hugged until the final call, hugged again, and then De and I turned and tried not to look back. We walked arm in arm for a while, sniffling and sighing.

"Hey, this is way too emotional," I told De. I didn't think I could handle it. If there was ever time for a little pick-me-up it was now. "You know, while I was looking for Tai's phone, I saw this great outfit around the corner from the souvenir shop."

De knew just what I was saying. "I'm there, Cher. I'm going to have to make some major purchases to put this one behind me."

So as Tai was taking off for the Big, Bad Apple, Dionne and I headed off for some fashion refreshment.

"She's gone?" Josh asked. "Just like that?" He tried to snap his fingers, but the butter from his popcorn made it impossible. One day he's going to learn to stay away from all that cholesterol.

I had a bowl of unbuttered next to me. Low cal. Good source of fiber. I'd taken my own suggestion to Tai about staying home in the romantic glow of the VCR. Josh and I had rented a video and curled up on my couch for a relaxing, romantic night in. "Yeah, she's gone. And after all the work we did on her," I said. "Like making a sand castle that gets washed away by the tide."

I stared at the TV set, but the movie wasn't cheering me up much. Part of the problem was, I'd given in to one of Josh's foreign films. Black and white with black subtitles that they seemed to have placed only on the black parts. No wonder they called it *film noir*. Like maybe if they kept you confused enough, you wouldn't realize that the movie wasn't any better than the kind they made around here.

"De and I had to tell Travis in school today."

"And?" For all his college-boy talk, Josh wasn't concentrating much on the movie, either.

"And he went seriously postal," I said. "Threw his skateboard against the lockers. Started screaming at me in the middle of the hall. He was all, 'Why didn't you stop her?' And 'Why didn't you call me?' A couple of teachers came by and took him off to calm him down. Good thing, or he might have thrown his skateboard at *me,* next. Struck down by a board full of Marvin the Martian stickers. I mean, grow up!"

Josh scrunched closer on the couch. "Count yourself lucky, Cher. I was reading that in ancient Greece they actually executed the messenger bringing the bad news."

"Don't you just hate history?" I said.

Josh laughed. "No. But let's talk about what I like." His voice went all low and soft. He brushed my forehead with his lips. He kissed me lightly on the mouth, and then more deeply. He fumbled around for the remote and clicked off the video. "Interesting flick," he said. "I'll have to check it out another time." Then he went back to what he'd been doing.

It wasn't going to be the same without Tai. But having Josh was a way excellent, all-natural pain killer.

Chapter 5

We missed Tai a lot. But we survived. Hey, we were young—we have a way of rolling with the punches.

Travis was the only one of us who really couldn't get it together. I mean, how many games of chicken on the Santa Monica Freeway could a guy survive? Especially on a skateboard. It was like with Tai, Travis had evolved way too quickly. Then Tai split, and bam, we had one more twelve-step casualty to deal with.

As for me, everything else was still pretty happening. On the plus side, Daddy had upped my allowance considerably. My grades had something to do with it—an A-plus from Geist-Hall and an A-minus from Hall-Geist. Or was it the other way around? Let's face it, those two were still letting me know how excellent things were between them, and I wasn't about to ruin a good thing. I was up near the top of the charts.

The other reason Daddy had raised my allowance was because we'd gotten his cholesterol level down from other planetary reaches. The twice-weekly tofu burgers, veggie juices, and nonfat frozen yogurt were working wonders.

But the real reason for my happiness was Boy One, Josh. We were on our third month already, and there was still no talk of divorce. I knew I'd found the perfect Baldwin.

"How about this one, Cher," Josh said. We were in his favorite campus bookstore. He reached up to the top shelf and pulled down a copy of *The Stranger*. "It's a classic, Cher. If Camus can't make you think, no one can."

Had I just been dissed? But Josh looked big-time earnest, convinced I was ready for some college-level, intellectual stimulation. I was perfectly happy with other kinds of stimulation, but if this made Josh happy, whatever.

I took the book from him and added it to the pile I was collecting. I'm way good at doing the big shop. I scanned the bookshelves for more loot. "Hey, I found one for you, Josh."

"As long as it doesn't have 'how to' and 'in less than thirty days' in the title, I'll consider it."

"After all this time you still think I'm an airhead," I said.

Josh stopped poring through the stacks and

turned to me. He wrapped his arms around me and gave a hug. "Cher, I just think you're ready for the advanced course in life. I mean all this stuff about you getting brainy and all. You know I'm half kidding. You know I already think you're—"

"Maybe it's not really you, Josh." I had to admit that the Tai situation had been bugging me again. "We had this terrible phone call last night. I just know she's not happy."

"Maybe it's the distance," Josh said.

"No. We're both cellular. It's like being in the next room, really," I told him. "It sounded like maybe she's up to her old tricks. She was all off on another solar system and stuff. Spaced, you know? For all I can tell she's back into that whole-herbal-refreshment-before-class routine. De thinks so, too."

"Even with your cellular you can't work miracles from three thousand miles away."

"I know," I said. "But it makes me seriously crazy to see one of my best projects fall apart. I mean, the only solution might be hopping a plane to New York and reeling her in."

"Don't you think you're exaggerating about Tai just a little? I mean, come on, Cher, you have to admit you do have a way with hyperbole."

"Moi? That's so totally false, Josh," I told him. "I really think Tai needs me again. Maybe I could just 747 it to the Big Apple and check up on her. Get in some shopping, while I'm there."

"Well, if you really think she needs you, that's probably the best way to find out. I suppose maybe you should go, Cher." Josh grabbed another book off the shelf. *"Being and Nothingness.* Sartre. For the plane ride."

"Can't you ever suggest *anything* uplifting?" I asked, adding the three-hundred-pound weight to my collection. "So you think I should go to New York? I mean, actually it's Tai who left us hanging. It's her life, and if she wants to do herself in, that's her prob. Besides, Josh, it sounds a little like you want to get rid of me for a while." I know I'd suggested it first, but I didn't love how totally casually he'd agreed to it. "Aren't I keeping you happy?"

"Don't make me dizzy, Cher." He handed me another hundred pounder and then treated me to a nice kiss on the mouth. "To put it in your terms, Cher, you make me way happy. I feel totally excellent when I'm with you."

I kind of wanted Josh to be his old sensible self and talk me *out* of going, not into it. But it did seem like the right thing to do. Tai was hopeless without me.

"Hi, Josh," a sort of familiar voice called out from behind us.

I turned around and—major ugggh! It was that existential girl from Drink Me. What timing.

"Hi, Simone," Josh said, sounding way friendly. "You remember my friend—"

"Don't tell me," she said, looking at me in that same condescending way she did at the cafe. "Zsa Zsa? Florence? No, Alice?"

"Cher. My name is Cher," I told her, unable to hide my iciness.

"Right. Cher. I knew it was one of those seventies TV people."

I noticed she had a stack of books under her arm. I scanned the authors. The usual suspects. Hegel, Kant, and more of that Nietzsche dude. What was it about that girl and philosophy? Was she always searching for meaning in her life? And why did she seem to think she was going to find it in my Josh?

I was speechless as she flirted up a storm with him. I checked out her hopeless outfit: 501s ripped in just the right place below the knee. The right place, that is, if you're living in 1991. The Birkenstocks were from the same century. And her thrift-shop halter left plenty of space to show off her sun-soaked waist and pierced belly button. Why did she have to be so cute?

When I came out of my stupor she was actually asking him out on a date, right in front of me.

"Tonight. Eight o'clock. It's on epistemology. I think it's called something like 'The Thought Process—Can We Really Know What We're Thinking?' You should come, Josh. It's going to be a hot lecture."

Spare me. Like you really needed a lecture to know what Simone was thinking.

"Yeah, well, maybe I'll make it. I don't know," Josh said.

Thank heavens she finally left or I might have gone totally wacko on her right there in the bookstore. The article in tomorrow's paper would have been called something like 'High School Betty Batters Thinking College Girl into Nonexistence.'

"Is there some reason you dislike Simone so much, Cher?" Josh asked me.

Hel-lo! "It wouldn't have anything to do with the fact that she's dying to take a chunk out of you," I told him, trying hard not to lose it completely.

"Give me a break, Cher. She's a classmate, period." Josh reached up for yet another book. "Now, what were we saying about your trip to New York?"

"As if! Like I'm really going to hop on a plane tonight with Miss Philoso-Fox hot on your trail."

Josh spun around to face me and scooped me up hard. The books we were collecting dropped out of my arms and crashed to the floor. He pulled me in and pressed his lips so firmly against mine I thought he'd suck me into oblivion. I was in the midst of one of the hottest kisses of my teendom. Right in public. But Josh wouldn't stop kissing me, and I didn't mind at all. Lose yourself in the moment, Cher. This is what life was really all about!

Finally we unlocked. "Need I say more to convince you who it is I'm interested in?" Josh asked.

I looked him right in his soulful brown eyes and

knew that he'd meant every kiss. "Do that again," I ordered.

While we embraced I let the wheels start turning. I just had to get home, make some plane reservations, pack a few bags, and get to the airport before Daddy could stop me. And I'd have to find De and convince her to come along.

"Hey, why stop now?" Josh asked as I pulled back.

I reached up on tiptoe and planted a soft one on his forehead. "Wait for me till I get back, hottie."

"I cannot believe you talked me into this," Dionne was saying. She speared a piece of lame-looking chicken with the cheap airline fork and watched the grease drip off of it. She made a disgusted face and dropped it back into its spot in the sectioned tray.

"Look, I'm sorry," I said. "I know you can't order the diet meal without twenty-four hours' advance notice, but Tai needs us *now*. I didn't think we should wait until tomorrow." I'd gone for the pasta primavera—gluey spaghetti and overcooked bits of veggies in library paste. And they only gave you this tiny little square-shaped pocket of it.

"Girlfriend, dinner's not the problem," Dionne said.

"It's not?" I asked in amazement. "Well, here then, have mine."

De made a face. "I mean, it *is* a problem. But it's not *the* problem. Hel-lo-o! What I'm trying to say is I can't believe you talked me into going to New York at all."

"But what about Tai?" I said. "De, we're her t.b.'s. If she can't count on us, who can she count on?"

Dionne shrugged. "But, Cher—New York City. You know what their motto is? 'Our city can kick your city's butt.' Two innocent girls from sunnier climes—aren't you scared?"

"Okay, De, so stay in L.A. and get zapped in a drive-by on the freeway," I said.

"Maybe I should have."

I tried to focus on the positive. I mean, being from California and all. "De—New York City, fashion capital of the world. Home of Donna Karan, Ralph Lauren, CK."

"You think they live in Brooklyn with Tai?" Dionne asked archly.

"De, I booked us a room in the middle of Manhattan. The Paramount Hotel. It's way chic. Christian told me all about it."

"Yeah?" De sounded only slightly appeased. "But, Cher, did you see how beautiful Beverly Hills looked when we flew over it? All those miniature swimming pools and tennis courts? They don't have that in New York."

"De, it's just for the weekend. When we get Tai back, we'll come home."

"And me and Murray—we haven't had a big-time blow-out in days. Actually, I'm a little worried. It just doesn't feel like a good time to leave him."

Bing! Bing! Alarms went off in my head. "I hear you there," I admitted. "Remember that girl in the coffeehouse? Simone?"

"Sure. 'Mental, Mental . . .' That about says it."

"But she *is* a Betty."

"Yeah, well, okay, she's all that," Dionne agreed.

I whapped De on the arm. "You didn't have to say so."

"Well, it's too late now," De said. "Of course we *could* just turn around when we get to New York and fly right back."

"As if! Tai's our friend, remember?" But Dionne had put a monster wrinkle in our mission. I pictured Josh and Simone in matching flannel, sitting close together at that lecture, as some oldster droned on about the meaning of life. I felt nervous. I felt sick. My neck was getting all warm and itchy.

"De. De," I said, flipping. "I'm getting a rash, right?" I put my fingers on my neck.

Dionne took one look and grimaced.

"I knew it!" I said. "Oh, no! And my supplies are down in the hold. I knew I shouldn't have let them check my makeup bag. I knew it."

"Cher, they have to check anything that won't fit under your seat," Dionne reminded me. "I'd let you borrow mine, but it might clash with the rest of your skin."

I groaned. Maybe I shouldn't have undertaken this rescue mission. Maybe I should have been selfish and stayed home. I pulled my cellular out of my Prada mini-knapsack. They hadn't been able to part me from that. "I've got to call Josh," I told De.

De wrinkled her forehead. "Wasn't your new telephone red, Cher?"

44

"Yeah, but this is my new, new phone. I gave the last one to Josh right before I left. So I could call him whenever. This one's guaranteed to many miles up in the air. Besides, I decided to do the basic black route this time, like the one I bought for Tai. It's so New York. And it does go with more."

"Go, girl!" De said. "You're gonna be buying those babies by the dozen soon."

"Good idea," I said. I can't resist a bargain. I punched in the number of the phone I'd given Josh. One ringy-dingy. Two ringy-dingies. Who said that? Some comedian I'd seen in reruns, I think. But it was not even a joke by six, seven, eight ringy-dingies. "Where is he?" I said desperately. I snapped the phone closed.

"Maybe he went out running," De said. Doesn't he do that health thing?

"De, why do you think they call it a mobile phone? He could take it with him when he goes running. You know how some people carry those little hand weights? Like that."

I felt way sorry for myself, so I drowned my sorrows in the pasta primavera, which had hardened into a gelatinous lump. Then I felt even worse. I calculated eight hundred calories, not to mention a bunch of ingredients found only in chemistry labs. I pinched my stomach. I could feel the rolls accumulating already. Eight hundred fat ones, all because Josh was out with a three-chord Betty.

My phone rang, startling me out of my woeful calorie count. The brain-dead guy across the aisle was momentarily startled out of his alcoholic stupor. Those little dollhouse-size bottles they have on airplanes can really add up if you work at it. I whipped the phone open.

"Josh? I knew you'd—"

"Guess again," Daddy said.

Whoops. I was toast. "Oh. Daddy. I was going to call you," I said.

"You were? Where are you? I can barely hear you. There's something wrong with this connection."

"Well, you know how you're always talking about what things were like back in New York?"

"I am?"

"Uh-huh." Then I broke the news to him as gently as I could.

I had to hold the phone away from my ear while he yelled. "You're going where!? Are you crazy? You're going three thousand miles away, to the most dangerous city in the world, and you didn't tell me?"

"I left you a note on the fridge," I said. "Daddy, Daddy, calm down."

"I will not!" he shouted. "Did we forget our little talk about those rooms at Snowbird?"

I felt a surge of disappointment. Or did the plane take a dip in altitude? But if giving up the deluxe suite at Christmas was the price of being a t.b. friend, I was going to have to accept it.

"You listen to me, Cher Horowitz. When you land in New York, I want you to get right back on the next plane to L.A.," came his voice, as I held the phone at arm's length.

"That's what I was saying," Dionne put in.

"Who's that? Cher are you listening?"

"Yes, Daddy, but our friend Tai needs our help. Besides—" Suddenly I had a brainstorm. Yes, Josh, I have smart ideas, too, I thought. "You're always telling me you'd give like a million dollars for those cookies from when you were a kid . . . those what do you call them?"

And it was Daddy, with the correct response in only two seconds. "Black and whites," he said. "From the Three Roses Bakery in the Bronx."

"Okay, so here's your chance," I said triumphantly. I didn't even add anything about how bad they were for his cholesterol level.

Daddy was silent.

"Daddy, don't worry about me. I'll be fine. It's only two days. I'll be careful, I promise. We're staying in a reputable hotel. And I'm not totally clueless . . ."

"You call me as soon as you get there," Daddy ordered.

"Yes, Daddy," I answered meekly.

"The Three Roses Bakery. No cheap imitations," he said.

"Not even," I promised.

Chapter 6

I'd caught a glimpse of Manhattan as we'd circled before landing. It was weird—I'd seen that view a million times in movies, TV, newspapers. So it was like I'd been here before. Except I hadn't. The Twin Towers, the Empire State Building, all the bridges leading to the heart of the city—and everything winking in the early morning sunshine.

Naomi Campbell was down there. Elle MacPherson. Cindy. Calvin Klein, too. Maybe even Naomi and Elle and Cindy *in* Calvin Klein. The thought was too intense. I was ready to parachute right down to fashion central.

And then there was Tai. Our own special native New Yorker. She was down there, too, and I couldn't stand to go much longer without seeing her.

It was way agonizing standing around the baggage area of the airport. I just wanted to get to the city. I watched the conveyer belt circle as we waited for our luggage to come out.

"Have you ever noticed that your own luggage is always the last to appear?" Dionne noted.

"Wow, you know, you're right," I said. "How do you think they manage to do that?"

I mean, it was only three pieces of luggage I was waiting for. Plus De's three. You know, enough for a little weekend trip. The worst was that I had to do my waiting in the same Armani mini I'd spent the whole flight in. My skirt was beyond wrinkled and looked deadly with my rash. To pass the time, I turned to Dionne and bemoaned the injustice of having to check every piece of makeup and clothing.

"Yeah, well, maybe it's like a bad sign or something," De said.

A lone, fake pony-skin suitcase came out way before anything else. No one stepped up to claim it. A planeload of sleepy, burnt-out-looking people followed it around and around with their eyes. Kind of like watching the wash cycle when there's nothing good on TV.

Then a few more bags appeared on the metal carousel. The crowd woke up. The woman who'd sat behind us on the plane hauled a large duffel off the moving belt. I kept a sharp eye out for my Louis Vuittons. I was not impressed with the quality of luggage on our flight. Some of it made Tai's Samsonite wannabes look elegant.

Meanwhile, somewhere out there behind the

glass exit doors, Elle and Naomi and them were climbing into one brutally fabulous outfit or other to start the day. I tried to smooth out my skirt.

"Cher—isn't that yours?" Dionne couldn't quite hide a note of excitement in her voice.

My big suitcase! What a beautiful sight all those tiny, gold, interlocking *L*'s and *V*'s were. I used my best aerobic technique to rush over and grab it. And then another of my bags was coming, and Dionne's tasteful, leather Coach bags were riding the conveyer, too.

We built up quite a pile next to us. I glanced around for a skycap. A young skinny guy in some drab-looking uniform was pushing an empty luggage cart at the edge of the crowd around the conveyer belt.

"Hello!" I called to him. I caught his eye. "Could you help us, here?"

He wheeled his cart over. "All this," I said to him. "Oh, and here. This is ours, too. And take this, and this . . ."

He was all "yes, miss, thank you, miss" as he loaded up all our luggage, adding my little backpack and De's shoulder bag that we'd carried onto the plane.

"Oh, wait, I can take that," I said, reaching out for the backpack. But he was already moving.

"Wait! Where are you going?" I called out.

"Taxi station, miss."

I was like, "whatever." I looked at De and we

started following him. Or tried to. But he was way fast.

Okay. You think we're major boneheads. Bimbos. Clueless. If it had happened to someone else, I'd probably think the same thing. I mean, come on—we're talking New York City. But believe me, it could happen to anyone. You've been up all night on the red-eye. Plus, your mind is on more important things. Like your close friend who you think may be in trouble. And your boyfriend who definitely will be in trouble if he's out with a certain discount Suzanne Vega imitation. And you're trying to imagine what all the most glamorous New Yorkers are getting dressed in that very second. I mean, there was a lot going on. Meanwhile, everything we had was taking off.

Which was how De and I wound up at the airport police station, with me talking to Daddy on the phone. A very unmobile deal right out of the Jurassic era, with one of those rotary dials and everything. Dangerous on a fresh manicure.

"So," Daddy said, "you told the nice man, 'here, take my things,' and he said, 'thank you,' and he did."

"Well, at least he was polite," I said.

But Daddy wasn't buying it. "Cher, my only daughter flies off into the night without so much as leaving me a note. She manages to get robbed before even setting foot outside the airport. Now about that immediate return flight back to L.A. . . ."

"Not even, Daddy. How could I live with myself if I turned around now, and Tai really needed my help?"

"And how are you going to live without yourself without a dime in the middle of New York?" Daddy countered.

I didn't have any trouble with that one. "You can wire us money. And express-messenger my new credit cards." I didn't give him a chance to say no. "Besides, De and I do have like this very little bit of money we were carrying on us," I rushed on. "About fifty dollars." Thank goodness for the Wonder Bra.

"A very little bit? When I was a boy in New York, that was a fortune," Daddy said.

Oh, that zing of elation! In his anger, Daddy had made a fatal tactical error. He'd always told me you had to stay level-headed when arguing a case. "Okay, so then we're not penniless. You said it first. No reason to come home."

"Cher! I'm not a patient man," Daddy said.

"I know that, Daddy. And you've been waiting for those black and whites for such a long time. When was the last time you were in New York?" I had him. I knew I did. "And as long as I'm already here, it would be such a shame to leave without them . . ."

The genuine antique of a phone was silent. Then Daddy sighed, and I was as good as strolling down Fifth Avenue already. Saks. Bendel's, Bloomie's. Wait, was Bloomingdale's on Fifth or Lexington? Drag city! The list Christian had made me was in my stolen bags!

"Okay, I'll wire some money to your hotel," Daddy said. "But you get me those black and whites if it's the last couple of dollars you have."

"Three Roses Bakery in the Bronx," I assured him. "I've got it all under control."

In my head, I was like, New York City, here I come.

In our fantasy trip, we would have been greeted at the airport by our limo driver with a major stretchmobile. Fully accessorized, of course— music, video, the works. If that didn't fly, we'd at least have hailed one of those yellow checker cabs, the ones with all that extra plush space to lounge around and act 1940s decadent.

But De and I went economy, and we had to reach into our bras to pay for the bus ride into Manhattan. Imagine. Me, Cher Horowitz, on the airport bus. How random.

Our vehicle was "sanitized for your riding pleasure." Eau de bus, like two parts Lysol, five parts Airwick Solid. That smell, and the fact that my Armani was wrinkling big time, made me feel totally tow-up. This was not the entrance to the fashion capital of the world I had hoped to make.

Still, I tried to put on that happy face. I wanted to have fun no matter what, and I had to get De pumped for the Big Apple, too. "This is so awesome, De! I mean here we are in New York."

"Big Apple," De said with a humph. "Try Rotten

to the Core. I mean, look at it out there, is that ugly or what?"

"Well—" What could I say? It wasn't pretty. Cracked sidewalks. Shabby little houses. The only glitter was the sparkle of broken glass in the street.

"Girlfriend, what colors do you see out this grimy window?" De asked.

"Gray, brown, and black. But what nice shades!" I tried. "Especially the gray."

"Hello! How about dirty, dirtier, and dirtiest."

"It's not all bleak," I said, still searching for a little color out there. "Litter. I see some colorful litter," I pointed out.

Sure enough, there was lots of that. Cans and bottles in every hue imaginable, and bigger things like car parts, bedroom sets, and bowling balls. The glam city we'd seen from the air was still a bus ride away.

We decided we'd do better to turn our attention inward, checking out our fellow bus riders in hopes of finding a Baldwin or two. Indeed, even on a lowly bus, the passenger list was *très* international. All shades were represented, though it was closer to the Far Side than a Benetton ad.

"Hey, De, what do you think of him?" I asked, pointing to a specimen a few rows in front of us. Bad-news outfit, but he had a killer smile. Definite potential.

De gave him the up and down. "Body of today, way yesterday dreadlocks. And thank you, but that's the stupidest lollipop shirt," she said. "But if you

54

strip him down and put him in a pair of Calvins we just might have a winner."

"What about him?" I asked, pointing to the guy sitting next to him. He looked more like a bean pole than a person. Pale gray complexion, totally bald, and he wore a metal earring that was so heavy it weighted his head slightly to the left.

"All-out Barney. No hope in the world," De said, breaking into a giggle.

The gal was finally laughing. Mission accomplished. I knew we could have a blast in New York, with or without cash.

We looked around at the rest of the collection of Fashion Freaks from Around the World. It was about a four-to-one Barney-to-Baldwin ratio. After we ran out of guys, we started checking out the gals, searching for a few Bettys amidst the Monets.

The one with the most potential was across the aisle from me. She could have been a drop-dead Betty. Cover girl of the month. Creamy smooth skin, near perfect bod, great smile, perfect teeth. But I wondered if she knew that her beret was on all wrong. I'd noticed it as soon as we'd gotten on the bus, and now I was starting to flip on it. This near perfect female needed my help.

De couldn't believe it when I leaned across the aisle and ever so diplomatically pointed to the beret. "Excuse me, but did you know that the band is showing?"

She gave me a curious look like "huh?"

"The band," I repeated. "You know, that leather

strap around your head. It's supposed to go on the inside. It's just not on right."

She still was looking at me like I was totally off. I realized we had a big-time communication gap. This goddess didn't speak a word of English. So I had to make lots of big swooping arm gestures to get my message across. Finally I just had to do it by my lonesome. I planted myself in the aisle and started rearranging. "You see, you've got these way excellent ears and you want to show them off, not cover them up." I did a little number with the thick, glossy dark hair peeking out from under the hat, too.

It just took a few seconds and then, voilà! Piece of cake. With my expertise, she'd gone from 9.5 to 10.

De gave me a congratulatory thumbs-up and the foreign babe gave me a righteous Colgate and thanked me in a thousand words I didn't understand.

And then New York City appeared, rising out of the bleak surroundings like a Baldwin in a sea of Barneys. The Empire State Building, the Twin Towers, that one that looked like a steel wedding cake with a huge spire on top. Whatever. This time I wasn't taking in the view of New York while a list of opening credits rolled. This was real. We were there!

Chapter 7

What do you suppose this is?"

De's voice rose over the sound of the Jacuzzi jets that were going full force on me. The curvy white porcelain tub could have fit eight comfortably. But for now, it was all mine. I'd need at least a half hour to get rid of all the eau de bus.

De was standing in front of the bathroom mirror, wrapped in a white towel. She was holding this weird white cylindrical thing in one hand, eyeing it suspiciously. "Too small for a coffee grinder and way too big for a lipstick holder," she said with a shake of the head. Then she twisted the top and out popped two funky-looking toothbrushes. "Hello!"

"Philippe Starck," I told her. "He did the whole hotel." I remembered Christian telling me all about the guy. He was like the architect of the moment, only he didn't just do floors and windows. Christian said his style was postmodern. I guess it meant he went postal on everything.

I was lathering up with some tangerine/almond/mint shampoo. I wasn't sure the stuff had even hit Beverly Hills yet. "Christian was right, De. This place is way today."

"Speaking of today, do you think you'll be out of the tub today? I mean, now that you've gotten me all the way here, I want to see the sights, okay? I confess. Besides, I gotta eat something soon or I'll die," De said.

"Okay, okay," I said. "But I was hoping the money and the plastic would hurry up and come so we could go all-out."

De left the room and called back in to me. "Girlfriend, remember I didn't touch a thing on that plane. I saw a Mickey D's around the corner. I could go for a burger with lettuce and tomato, hold that way caloric beef and bun."

Ugh. Here we were in New York City, and De was having a Big Mac attack. As if.

But before the words were out of my mouth, De was all "Whoa! Eighty-six that Big Mac. Cher, you gotta check out what's happening in the mini-fridge." I could hear her taking inventory, and I realized I could go for a snack, too.

I toweled off and joined De in the main room. She'd laid out this awesome-looking buffet. Way high in calories, but worth the splurge—runny

French cheeses, trendy crackers, an unbelievably fancy jar of beluga caviar, and two bottles of Evian.

We went at it in a big way. All eat now, pay later. "I'm starting to like this New York thing, girlfriend," De managed between bites. "Hey, let's drink a toast. To our view." She raised her Evian to the symphony of glass and steel outside the window. "And to getting out there and seeing it."

We clinked Evians and toasted to the bright lights and big city that stood before us.

"And to our mission to bring back Tai," I added. Along with getting our plastic and buying up the town.

"I'm with you there," De seconded.

"Maybe I should call downstairs and see if the provisions have arrived."

"Nothing yet, Ms. Horowitz. But you are expecting it soon, yes?" I recognized the voice of the guy who'd checked us in. Barney with an attitude. I knew snooty and I knew nasty. I think there was both in his voice. I mean, hel-lo. Hadn't he noticed I was wearing Armani? And De was like one-hundred-percent Versace. He couldn't possibly have thought we were faking it, just for a free suite. Some people!

"I wonder if something happened to Daddy. Maybe he got so busy at work he just spaced." I started dialing Daddy from the room phone. I was so used to autodial on my cellular, I couldn't believe how long it took to punch in those numbers. "Busy. It figures." I dialed again, but the same. Then I thought I should call Josh. Maybe he'd know what was up. But I hesitated.

"Cher, could be this thing you have about Josh and the Mental, Mental girl is all made up. Just call him," De said.

So I did. The phone rang and rang and rang. And I was sorry De had made me call, because now I was really flipping that the Mental, Mental girl was getting way existential with my boyfriend.

But then I replayed the kiss in the bookstore. Melt city. Maybe I was getting worked up over nothing. Too bad Josh couldn't be here. We'd head straight for one of those Central Park horse-and-buggy rides and tell the driver to circle the park a bunch of times.

But what was he doing instead? And the worries came flooding back.

De decided that a taste of the Big Apple would take my mind off all that. So we did up the final crumbs of our feast and got ready for a trip to Tai's. Except I wasn't going anywhere with this monster grease stain on my cropped T-shirt.

"It's not that bad, Cher," De lied unconvincingly.

Then it came to me in a flash, a vision. There was this funky-chic piece of cloth draped over one of the chairs in the room. It was kind of like an African print, with lots of reds and oranges. You know that designer thing, lightly tossing something colorful over a stark white chair. I picked it up, decided the colors were happening with my skirt, and made a kind of Me-Jane thing, wrapping it around my top and knotting it just above my navel, showing lots of skin.

"Go, girl," De said with an approving whistle. "How about this for me?" She grabbed one of the Paramount Hotel cloth napkins and gave it a yank. "Shhh, promise you won't tell," she said as she tore off a narrow piece and made it into a trendy head band.

"Do it yourself," I said with satisfaction. The lack of makeup was a major problem, but I pinched my cheeks for a little color and told myself we could raid Tai's stash as soon as we got to her place. Way good thing we'd sent her home with some quality supplies.

We gave each other a limp five and headed out for Tai's approval. I only wished Josh could have seen me.

"You gotta stop buggin'," De told me as we went down in the hotel elevator. "He could be anywhere."

"Yeah, like anywhere in her dorm room," I said. "I bet she's got one of those Indian hippie bedspreads up on her window instead of curtains."

De shook her head sympathetically. "So Woodstock Nation. I mean, I sort of like those hip-hugger pants they wore, but . . ."

"But how could my Josh have such random taste?" I wailed. "De, you think he's with her, too. Spill it."

Dionne shrugged. "All I know is, *you* wanted to come here. You could have stayed with him. I could be fighting with my man, right now. So forget about him and remember why we're here."

For a second, I thought about all the way happening shops and stores out there, and how the only plastic we had was—well, De says her hair extensions are all natural, but I'm not entirely sure.

But then a picture of Tai popped into my head. Tai, as we'd first seen her, with the red and purple streaks in her hair. And the shapeless jeans and dirty sneaks. Tai, who'd shown up on the shores of sunny California needing some big help. I felt a wave of resolve. I had a purpose here. I wasn't going to let Josh and that thin-voiced, existentially challenged, neo-pseudo-hippie—

"Ooh!" I went, flipping in a major way. "How," I asked, as the elevator door slid open, "can I forget about Josh when . . . when . . . um . . ."

Every thought poofed right out of my head as I took in the view. Against the shimmery gold wall of the hotel lobby, posing under hot spotlights in the eye of a camera, was one exceptionally, righteously, chronically capital-B Baldwin. And I knew him. I mean, not personally, but I'd seen him before. In magazines and stuff. Like that first view of Manhattan. Only more. *The* New York moment. I couldn't have dreamed it up better myself.

Somehow I floated out of the elevator and over to the photo shoot. "De," I whispered. "De, do you see what I see?"

"Doable," Dionne said. "If you like that long-haired type."

"If?" Long-haired, short-haired, the guy was a babe. Sun-streaked locks, big baby blues, perfect Soloflex body.

Then he looked at me and smiled. No, he did. And then the photographer was all "take five while we reload," and I don't know how it happened, but we were moving toward each other, and it was so sudden, but it was like slow motion at the same time. And then we were standing right there together in the lobby of the hotel, and he was still smiling at me, and I was all, like, oh, my god, what do I say . . .

"You're the cover model from *GQ*, aren't you?"

He nodded. "And I recognize you from . . . that *Mademoiselle* spread, right?"

As if! I shook my head slowly. "I'm not a model," I said.

He made this totally adorable frown, and his thick, sandy-colored eyebrows came together. "You're not? Oh, wow. Well. You could be."

"I could?" Cindy, Nikki, and me.

"Sure. Hey, great shirt. Oh, listen—I'm Griffin." He extended his hand.

I took it, and he clasped on with his other hand, too, and, like, sort of held my hand in his for a few seconds. I mean, we were standing there with all these people and all these cameras and we were holding hands!

And he was like "and you are . . . ?"

Major embarrassing. We're holding hands, but

I'm so starstruck that I've forgotten to introduce myself. "Cher. Cher Horowitz."

"Cher. Like in the infomercials."

I nodded. We understood each other right away.

"So, are you staying in this hotel?" Griffin asked.

I nodded. "I'm visiting from L.A."

"As in Hollywood? Films? The big screen?"

I nodded.

"You have anything to do with all those stars?" Griffin asked.

"Well, my father's worked with a bunch of them," I said.

"Yeah? Wow, I can dig that."

Then the blissful moment was broken as the photographer called out Griffin's name. "Well, I gotta get back to work," he said. "But listen, I'm doing a runway show at Saks this afternoon. Usually I do print work, but this is a special gig—lots of big-name folks there. Why don't you come check it out?"

"Really?" I was all squeaky.

"Sure. See you there," Griffin said. He gave me this outrageous wink and went back to the gold wall. A demigod against a shimmering, shining sky.

And then, well, you know how it is. First it was like De was there, and then I spied Griffin and everyone kind of disappeared, even though I guess De was basically next to me the whole time, and then there she was again, and I was sort of leaning on her, and my heart was pounding. Whatever.

"That happened, right?" I breathed. "He talked to

me. He thought I was a model. He touched me. We have, like, this sort of date, this afternoon."

"Chill, girlfriend," she advised. "I seem to remember something about someone named Josh . . ."

"Oh. Well, he's got Miss Indian Print Bedspread. And didn't you just tell me to forget about him?" But she'd already popped my balloon. Well, maybe not all the way popped. Maybe let out a little of the air.

"And don't forget that we have a previous date to rescue Tai."

"Tai. Sure. Of course. But we can go to the show at Saks, too. All of us. Me, you, and Tai. Like the old days."

De shrugged and made the big *W* for whatever.

"Wait, De. You don't think that Griffin's—well, you remember what happened with Christian."

Call me lost. I'd had kind of a major crush on Christian for a few days, until Murray had clued me in that I'd never, ever have what it took to make Christian happy. It was better that way. Christian and I were total pals now. But Griffin . . .

"Not even," De assured me, easing up on me a little. "I saw the way he was looking at you. And, girl, he thinks you're a Betty."

"He does?"

"You know it," said De, and then we were all giggling and stuff and I was *so* totally pleased that we hadn't turned around at the airport and gone right back to Beverly Hills.

Chapter 8

*I*t was harder to hold on to that sunny feeling thirty feet under. The subway shook and made this metallic clatter and squeal that was definitely way hazardous to the health of my ears. It wasn't a healthy meal for my eyes, either. A scrawny person inside a bundle of rags was crashed out in one corner of the car. A walking ad for Budget World's bargain basement sat across from us, calmly and publicly picking her nose. A trio of tough guys took up one whole long bench. You know, the kind of dudes who probably think getting a tattoo feels a little like being tickled. One of them had like this entire aquarium of reptiles reproduced on his bare bulky arms. I tried hard to look like I wasn't looking at him.

Next to me, De was wound tight as a Lycra

bodysuit. "I think I heard that they kill tourists down here for fun," she said through clenched teeth. She kind of whispered it and yelled it at the same time, so I would hear her over the noise of the moving train.

"Take a chill pill, De. It's just a bunch of people going to visit friends or on their way to work or stuff." Well, maybe there *were* one or two people who looked as if they might have been gainfully employed at some point in their lives. But one had his face buried in a newspaper and the other was staring up at an ad for hemorrhoid medicine as if it were the most fascinating thing he'd ever read. See no evil, hear no evil, speak no evil. If one of the thugs decided to use us for target practice, we were Jarlsberg cheese.

As the train squeaked into the next station, I resisted the temptation to get off. Pick-a-nose made her exit, touching the door sill with the same hand that had been doing the digging. When I *did* get off, I'd use the other set of doors.

I felt overexposed in my fabulous Philippe Starck tablecloth cum halter. I kind of wrapped my arms around my waist and tried to cover up as much skin as possible. No hope. And my bare legs were sticking to the hard plastic seat. No way Elle and Kate and them traveled by subway.

Still, the thought of Tai at the other end of this ride reminded me why we were doing this. Tai. She needed us. And we needed her.

We continued our authentic New York transit

experience, bouncing through a long, dark tunnel. We made a few more stops. The newspaper reader got off, leaving his paper on his seat. Someone else got on, tore off a piece of the paper, and started using it to wipe something unspeakably gross off her sneaker.

I tried studying the hemorrhoid ad. "Mr. Vargas sits all day long," the ad read. Mr. Vargas looked major miserable. Talk about pains in the you-know-where. And then there was the ad next to that. The woman on that poster looked as unhappy as Vargas. "It's only ten o'clock and already her back aches," it said. An ad for Motrin? Some other backache relief? Guess again. It was an ad for a doctor specializing in breast reduction. I pondered that one for a minute. Reduction?! Wow, they sure had a different way of doing things here than they did in Hollywood.

I memorized the rest of the ads, as well as the mystery stains on the dirty floor. We made one stop after another. DeKalb Avenue, Atlantic, Seventh. When was this ride going to be over?

The one tough guy was flexing his snakes and lizards. I started getting this awful feeling. Like what if we were on the wrong train? "Where were we supposed to get off? Sheep-shead Bay?" I asked De.

De nodded. "There's a map over there," she said.

Right next to Snakeskin. Chronic. I looked at De, but she wasn't moving. I took a breath and stood up. I could feel the tough guys looking at me. I tugged on my skirt, trying to make my mini a tiny bit more maxi. I kept my eyes fixed on the subway map in its

Plexiglas case. A graffiti signature was scrawled over one corner of it. I got up close enough to take a look. A mess of long, twisty, colorful lines spread all over the boroughs of New York. Was our train represented by the red line? The blue one that split off into four different directions at one end and two at the other. I didn't have the slightest idea where we were. Had we already crossed from Manhattan into Brooklyn?

Then I felt someone right behind me, and my heart skipped as I saw the inky reptiles on his arms. He was all "where are you going?" And he kind of stared at the map along with me.

Oh, my god. He wanted to know where we were getting off. No, he wasn't going to use us for target practice down here in the subway. He was going to wait and do it somewhere more private. Should I ignore him? How could I? He was standing so close I could hear him breathing. Make up a destination? He'd catch me in my lie and it would be that much worse.

"Sheep-shead Bay?" I said in this teeny-tiny voice.

He laughed. "Sheepshead." He pronounced it Sheep's Head.

"Oh," I said.

"So yuz ain't from around hea."

"Huh?"

"You 'n' ya goilfrien'." He threw a glance at De, who was frozen and petrified in her seat. "Wheh yuz from?"

"Oh," I repeated. "Uh, California?" I managed.

"L.A.?" I was probably breaking a cardinal rule of New York subway travel. Never, ever give out personal information. But what could I do?

"L.A.? I gotta cousin moved out deh," he said. "Bobby Zucca." Pause. "Ya don't know him? Bobby Z.?"

As if! I shook my head.

Snakeskin actually looked disappointed. "It's a big city," I said. "Like New York." I started studying the map again.

Snakeskin moved in and jabbed a finger at a spot at the edge of the map. "Sheepshead Bay. It's a bunch maw stops."

Maw? Oh, *more.*

"We get off duh stop befaw, so you'll know."

"Thanks," I said. Was it possible I'd misjudged this guy?

"Yeah, Jimmy ova deh, he had a goilfrien' lived in Sheepshead." He nodded at one of his friends. "Yo, Jim—dese ladies gonna Sheepshead."

"Yeah? Oh, man, Vincenzo's Clam House!" Jimmy yelled across the subway car. "Gotta check it out! Umbul-lievable fried calamari."

Fried? Well, maybe they could just grill them and give them a squeeze of lemon. De and I exchanged surprised looks.

Anyway, by the time Snakeskin and company got off the subway, we were actually kind of sorry to see them go. And I was even getting to be able to understand the foreign language they spoke. "See?"

I told De. "There wasn't a thing to get freaked about."

Even De had to admit that maybe New Yorkers weren't as unfriendly as she'd thought. And hey, how many of our classmates back in Beverly Hills had ridden the D train almost to the end of the line?

It was kind of amazing that we actually did get to Tai's house. The subway was like you go down in this dark hole for about half a lifetime, then it's finally over and you resurface for air and you find out you've only traveled about two miles. In the same amount of time I could have driven from Beverly Hills to Palm Springs. If I had my license, I mean.

Anyway, De and I stood in front of a tiny little brick house with the paint peeling off the front door. Tai's house looked exactly like every other one on the block. Each one was attached to the next, and it would have been kind of quaint in someone else's movie. There was a group of kids playing baseball right in the street and another gang of older guys, toasted and just hanging out sitting on some cars. Those guys were way disgusto because they did their whistling routine at De and me when we walked past them. All "whoa baby, you're my type" and "my place or yours?" Oh, and one guy actually called me fat. Outrageous!

We rang her bell, and there was this instant sound of two dogs barking. They were the yapping kind, so we readied ourselves for two little toy-size terriers. You know, the kind that look more like rats.

"Tai didn't say anything about dogs," De said, backing up a step. "You know I'm allergic."

"Chill, De, you'll be fine. Remember, Tai needs us." It was not going to be a pretty sight if one of those dogs started nipping at De, because knowing her, she'd go postal, too.

"Who's dare?" a kid's voice that sounded exactly like Tai called out from behind the door. We knew we were in the right place.

"We're friends of Tai's from Beverly Hills," I shouted over the barking.

We heard the sound of a lock turning. Then another and then another and yet another. You just hoped they never had a fire in there and had to get out fast. Finally, the door was pulled open a peep, the chain still on. A little boy stared out at us. "Beverly Hills? Where's dat? In duh Bronx?"

De and I could hardly believe it. Was this a made-for-TV movie or what? But the little boy was a dollface. He looked like a mini Sly Stallone minus a few thousand muscles, and it was way cute that he was trying to protect the house.

"California," De explained. "You know, like, Hollywood, the Dodgers, Mickey Mouse."

"Yeah, okay, but I shouldn't let ya in. Cuz my mother says no strangers or nuttin."

"Well, maybe you could just get Tai for us, then you'll see we're not strangers," I said.

"Yeah, okay," he said. Then he stopped and thought it over for a minute. "Nah, Tai's gonna kill me if I wake her up. Nah, you bettah do it." Then he undid the chain and let us in.

What a case. It got even stranger when the boy went right to the tape deck and shut off the recording of the barking dogs.

"She's upstairs. First daw on da left."

De and I headed up the stairs not sure what we were in for next. We gave a little knock and let ourselves in.

"Uh-huh, not a moment too soon," I said, as I looked in on our friend in need. Tai was fully clothed. Not like in a nightie or even comfy pajamas, but I mean there she was in her 501s. The same way baggy pair she wore the first day we met her in Beverly Hills. Flannel shirt, hiking boots, everything. The only thing she wasn't wearing was makeup.

Flat-out crashed right on top of her mismatched sheets and pillow cases. But it was way wonderful to see her face. In that second, I realized how much I'd missed her.

We went over to her and tapped her, De on one side, me on the other. Tai had this everything's-just-way-groovy look on her face as De and I kind of batted her back and forth in a major effort to wake her.

Finally her eyes opened and she gave us her famous sleepy Tai smile. "Hey, you guys. What's up?"

"Like, hi, girlfriend," De said.

I gave her a little wave and a smile. "Hi, Tai. Like we missed you."

Then Tai's eyes opened huge. "Huh? Like, wow! Oh, my—you guys are really here! In my room! Umbuh-lievable!" True to form, she nearly fainted. De and I sat on her bed, holding Tai up between us, taking turns fanning her.

"I don't get it. What are you guys doing here? You really came all this way?" Tai asked, still foggy.

"We just felt like checking you out, Tai," De said.

"But it's like three thousand miles."

"You're worth it, Tai," I said. "Besides, De and I both wanted to add on some frequent-flyer mileage."

"If I knew you were coming I could have planned a whole New York vacation for you," Tai said. "Why didn't you tell me?"

"We wanted the surprise advantage," I said.

"Advantage?"

"De and I thought we'd find out what the big deal was about you and New York. You know, like, we wanted to check out why you really left Beverly Hills."

"Oh," Tai said. She totally paused. It was like now she was awake and things were beginning to register. "Like I told you guys, I needed the freedom. And I definitely made the right choice splitting Beverly Hills. I mean, I really miss you two and all, but things have been excellent here. Everything's just the way I want it."

De and I looked at each other, eyebrows raised. If

Tai's bedroom was any indication of the way her life was going, then it wasn't going anywhere too fast. It made me think of those *Odd Couple* reruns with that slob, Oscar Madison. He was a New Yorker, too. I wondered if that's where Tai got her decorating schemes.

But it didn't seem like a good idea to push Tai too much all at once. Not when she was still pretending that everything was way awesome. Best to do some serious hanging—get Tai remembering what she'd left behind in California, then hit her up with the thought of coming back west. De was on my same wavelength.

"So are you going to get out of bed and show your California pals the sights?" De asked, all casual and stuff. "After all, we are tourists."

"You mean like the Empire State Building and the Statue of Liberty?" Tai asked.

"We were thinking more along the lines of Fifth Avenue. Trump Tower, Tiffany's, Bloomie's," I told her.

"Yeah, I guess," Tai said, but she hardly seemed pumped. "I don't know, I'm supposed to meet my posse in the Village."

"Posse? I thought we were in New York, not Dodge City," I said.

De reminded me that *posse* was a street thing. A word that Murray liked to use. Not that the boy knew squat about hanging on the street—unless you counted the long, winding private road that led to his Beverly Hills estate.

Whatever. "Look, Tai, we came all the way here to see you," I said. "I mean, I'm taking a major chance leaving Josh all alone back in Beverly Hills. I've put my romantic interests way in jeopardy for you. Now, how about Saks Fifth? There's a great fashion show later this afternoon that I'm expected to show for."

"Cher's hit it big already," De explained to Tai. "Cher, tell her about your new friend. Grant? Bettencourt? What was his name again?

"Excuse me for getting noticed. De's just jealous because this really cool model kind of checked me out. His name's Griffin, and he's major Baldwin material."

"That part's true, I'll admit," De said.

"You'd probably recognize him, Tai. Anyway, we met him at the hotel, and he spotted me right away. He seemed pretty sure I had what it took to be a supermodel," I said. I mean, that was what had happened, wasn't it?

Supermodel. It sounded strange. But it sounded totally awesome, too. The whole world already knew about Naomi, Veronica, Christy, and Cindy. Could I possibly be next?

As I floated off into daydreamland, De and Tai were making plans to meet Tai's posse before hitting the stores. I suppose it made sense, seeing that we'd come all this way for Tai. Besides, without our charge cards back, we couldn't really shop yet, anyway.

"You guys will love where we hang. Washington

Square Park—it's like real famous and all," Tai announced proudly.

De's ears perked up. "That's where Murray wanted me to get him his neck piece. He heard about this guy who carves real way-out African stuff. You know how my man is, he just gets it in his head somehow that there's this one guy in the whole world who's authentic.

"Whatever," I said. "I suppose it's worth a look."

"Cool," Tai said. She got up off the bed and sort of pulled up her jeans and pulled down her shirt all in the same motion. "We're Audi."

I grimaced slightly at the notion of Tai going out on the town looking like that. We had to at least do her face—and ours, too. Okay, Tai's colors weren't mine—and they certainly weren't De's—but she had a few lipsticks and eye pencils that would do in a pinch.

A little while later, we were ready to Audi into the world. Okay, Tai still had on her ratty jeans, but the important thing was that we were all together. De and I had the whole weekend to work our charms on Tai. I was sure that it was just a matter of time before we had her back in full Beverly Hills style.

I gave Tai a huge hug, funky clothes and all. De got in on the act, and we all did this jumping-up-and-down kind of huddle and we threw in a bunch of squeals and stuff, because it was so righteous to be a threesome, again. Operation Get Tai Back was under way.

Chapter 9

*W*ashington Square Park is at the very bottom of Fifth Avenue. The same Fifth Avenue that farther uptown is home to none other than Saks Fifth Avenue. But don't let the common avenue fool you. You walk through this huge arch on the north end of the park, and you see right away that the folks hanging here wouldn't know a quality label from, well, a tablecloth. Not that they weren't an interesting mix. But talk about yesterday, this place was Neanderthal—maybe even older. Hippies, toast products, rasta heads, skateboard slackers, beat poets, artistes, you name it, they were out there in full force. It was like a contest over who had longer hair, dirtier jeans, and less of a clue that we were nearing the year 2000.

"So, like, what do you guys think?" Tai asked as we took in the scene. "Way cool, huh?"

De and I had stopped dead in our tracks. "It's way something, that's for sure."

"Yo, Tai. Zup?" This guy who looked like a cross between a Martian and an electric eel welcomed us. He had a pale green face and wild neon blue hair that stuck straight up. Creative, I'll admit, but he needed some editing.

Tai's posse was hanging out in the middle of the park, near a huge fountain that was not presently spouting a single drop of water. I wasn't sure if Tai's friends were hippies disguised as grunge or the other way around. There were at least ten different wasters strumming out-of-tune guitars, one half attempting Dylan, the other half failing at Nirvana. And the few who weren't playing music or zoning were playing the lamest game of hackeysack you'd ever seen.

"Zup, everybody? Hi, Lenny," Tai said, giving a kind of embarrassed smile to an extra toasty skinny guy with a mop of soft black curls. He was one of the hackeysackers, pretty excellent with a bean bag, but what did that really mean?

"She left Beverly Hills for this?" De whispered to me.

I shrugged and gave her the whatever sign.

"Yo, it looks like Tai brought some new scenesters. Like, you guys gonna hang out and chill with us?" another one of the posse asked.

As if. "Actually, we just stopped by for a moment. To see this downtown thing. Then we're hitting some of the other sights—Bergdorf's, Saks . . ." I made it perfectly clear that we were Audi ASAP.

"Sax? Did she say she plays the sax?" Lenny asked. "Cool."

"Nah, dude, I think she meant Saks Fifth, like uptown where my mama shops," Mr. Blue Hair from Outer Space said.

The posse did a group giggle, at least they made an effort to laugh, but it came out way lame.

"Hey, come on," Tai protested. "Be nice. These are my friends. Cher and De. They're from Beverly Hills. They're cool, okay?"

"Yeah, and we live in the present, too," I informed them.

"Hey, the present's whatever you make of it, Cherskie."

"Cherskie?" The nerve of that blue martian. "And what's your name? Hairskie?"

"Actually it's Wilson."

"Wilson Tyler Stratton," Lenny added.

"The third," another posse-mate chimed in.

You've never seen a green face turn so red so fast. "Whatever," Wilson mumbled.

Whatever? Now, there was a line I could relate to.

"All right, like I'm sorry, okay?" Wilson said. "Any friend of Tai's—"

Mr. Wilson Whatever the Third sounded sincere enough, so I decided if Tai liked him he was probably okay. And maybe the guy did have a point about everybody living in the here and now. Or maybe I was just lightening up a little, digging the scene, as they say. If I wasn't careful I could turn to toast by osmosis.

"So what about that African dude and his carvings?" De wanted to know.

Lenny knew who she meant. "Melon Head. Yeah, he's right over there. He's the master. Come on, I'll introduce you."

While Lenny, Tai, and De went over to find something for Murray, Wilson the Third and I continued to explore the depths of our cross-continental differences.

"So what's a way phat dope girl like you doing in the Big Apple, anyway?" he wanted to know.

I was stunned. I thought he was becoming my pal, and now I was the butt of his latest put-down. And it was the second time today I'd been called fat!

"Like what *is* your real problem, anyway?" I said. "FYI, stoner, I'm at the top of my class, so I'm no dope. And as far as fat goes, I challenge you to find one single ounce of cellulite on my entire bod. That doesn't mean you can touch, but look. Note the outfit. You just don't pull off a mini this short, and the exposed navel if you've got excess baggage. Not only that, but I'll have you know I've only been in New York a few hours and I've already been discovered." Well, just about. Griffin *had* mistaken me for a model. "You are looking at the cover girl of the near future, okay? And let me tell you, Mr. Wilson Whatever Your Name Is the Third with the Way

Retro hairstyle, street urchins don't whistle disgusto comments like 'yo, sexy' and 'mmmmmmmm' at fat girls."

Wilson Three just looked at me like I'd totally bugged out. Then he was all laughing like a hyena and stuff. "Dope? Fat? Oh, man. You thought I was dissing you? What a trip. Hey, I thought you said you were from the present."

He told me that *dope* meant "excellent" and that "fat" was really *phat*, like with a *P*, and it was like his East Coast way of saying I was a Betty. I could only blush when I realized.

"So you think my do is whack," Wilson said.

"Translation?" I asked, reminding him that I spoke Californian.

"My spikes," he said pointing to his blue hair. "You called them retro. So what's wrong with them?"

"Look, why go for, like, two decades ago when you could have something totally now?" I asked him.

"You wanna give me a couple of mad ideas?"

"Mad?" I asked.

"Dope, I mean. Phat, you know, way excellent in your language," he said. "Come on, do me up, Cherskie," he said.

The next thing I knew, I was back on the job. Wilson's hair was stiff and sticky. He said he did a post-shampoo with beer and sugar. Frankly, it made a mean hair gel, and it smelled kind of nice, too. Maybe he was onto something.

While I was considering various styling possibilities, I found out that the Third part of his name referred back to his grandfather, Wilson Tyler Stratton, Numero Uno. It turns out that Gramps didn't have blue hair, but he did invent a certain product that made him among America's hundred richest men in the world. Which meant that Wilson wasn't doing so badly himself. Except that he swore that when the big inheritance day came, he was going to go to the top of the Empire State Building and dump the whole lot out the window.

"All eight hundred and fifty-nine million of it. In ones and fives," he said. "Really I will."

Getting the D.L.—that's N.Y. speak for down low, like the whole truth and nothing but—gave me inspiration. I decided if I gave the neon blue locks a more traditional styling, it just might be the perfect combo for him, one part wastoid, one part Brahmin. So I matted the spikes down, brushed—or rather raked them to one side—and gave his hair a little upturn on the ends. He would never look Banana Republic, but it did add a certain degree of class, which he definitely deserved.

"Whoa, you look great, dude," Lenny said as he, Tai, and De made their way back to us.

De was holding a way dope necklace with some funky carvings of African gods and goddesses that I knew would look totally phat on Murray. De slapped me a limp one when she saw how I'd transformed Wilson. "And I thought there wasn't much hope. Girlfriend, you are a miracle worker."

"Cher is the queen of makeovers," Tai agreed. "She did me back in Beverly Hills," she told her posse. "It was so great!"

Key word—was. Tai needed a serious touch-up, that was for sure. If we didn't get her back to Beverly Hills fast, she was going to be just another neo-pseudo-nouveau-hippie-punk. Whatever.

Still, it was a beautiful, crisp, sunny day. Okay, more crisp than anything else, if you figured in the company. But it wasn't so painful to hang out and be entertained by the neo-pseudo crowd. We requested our favorite oldies from the guitar players, watched a few good skateboard moves, and got to see *le tout* downtown parading through the park: college students, artists with paint-splattered jeans, suits stealing a few moments out of the office, bike messengers with their huge canvas shoulder bags, parents with little kids.

Wilson played tour guide. "See her?" He pointed to a woman in a steel blue suit with a fitted jacket and a knee-length skirt, walking quickly through the park. Not a bad outfit, especially in this sea of trash-fish. "Publishing," Wilson said confidentially. "Editor or maybe in the publicity department. She's on her way to her therapist."

"How can you be so sure?" De asked.

Wilson shrugged. "Hang around long enough, you just know. Him?" A guy in sweats and a leather jacket. "Student. Majoring in business, but he really wants to be an actor."

It was actually a good way to see the real New

York. Or part of it. But as it got toward lunchtime, we made a move. My new blue-haired pal was fun, but it was definitely time to hit the fancier part of town.

We scooped up Tai and said our goodbyes. To everyone, that is, except Lenny and his hackeysack bag. Wouldn't you know that he couldn't take a hint. He decided to tag along, and Tai didn't seem to have the heart to talk him out of it. Well, at least we hadn't left Tai back at the fountain. She was with us now. Where she belonged. We just had to figure out how to keep it that way.

Chapter 10

A couple of minutes of underground black-hole transport and whoosh! Downtown became Uptown, a change as awesome as flipping from the Home Shopping Network to *Melrose Place*.

Fifth Avenue was nothing short of glitz and glamour. Wall-to-wall beautiful people. Everywhere you looked it was high fashion, fancy eateries, museums and art galleries, and totally to-die-for stores.

This was my kind of New York. And it offered mega amounts of my favorite sport—shopping. But let's face it, it was a sport that you needed the big bucks for, which at the moment I didn't have. Just looking at all the bags making their way up and down the avenue—Bloomies', Bendel's, Tiffany's, Ann Taylor, and, yes, Saks—I could barely control myself. But De kept reminding me to stay calm till the cash and plastic got wired to us. Then we'd go ballistic.

"How's your red hot?" Tai asked.

"Huh?" I was so busy drooling over all the style on the street, I'd forgotten I was holding a mustard-drenched hot dog in a limp doughy bun. Don't get me wrong, I actually like hot dogs. That is when I'm eating them poolside in Beverly Hills as part of a Fourth of July barbecue bash. It's a whole other thing to be munching on a weiner while eyeing the Rich and Famous on their way to four-star lunches.

"Uggh" was about all I could manage as I eyed my red-hot with a great deal of suspicion. Okay, so I finally took a bite and it was surprisingly delish. Still, I wasn't about to admit it. I mean, right across the street was the Russian Tea Room, only one of New York's fanciest. How could I show emotion over a hot dog when people were in there stuffing themselves with smoked salmon, roast duckling, and blini with caviar?

De, meanwhile, had wolfed down her hot dog and was on to seconds. She was having it New York style, heavy on the caramelized onions and sauerkraut. It had to be way caloric, but she balanced it out with a bottle of zero-fat Evian. Even so, De was going to need to do a double dose, *Buns of Steel* as well as Kathy Smith's step workout, when we got back to Beverly Hills.

"How about you, Cher?" Lenny asked me. "Let me buy you another."

For toast, I suppose Lenny was really okay. I mean he'd treated us all to lunch. And it had cost him half a day's salary from his job as a baseball-cap vendor at Yankee Stadium.

I managed to resist another dog, but I took him up on a second Evian.

"You sure you don't want a Yoohoo instead of the water?" he asked.

Yoohoo was like chocolate milk with extra sugar and unpronounceable chemicals. Tai and Lenny swore it was awesome, but De and I stuck to the clear stuff. Okay, so we were eyeing the Yoohoos with major envy, but if you wanted to keep your figure and avoid cancer you just had to draw the line somewhere, right?

"Hey, check this out. I'll show you guys some of my moves," Lenny said. He gave Tai his bottle of Yoohoo and was off, zigzagging his way up the sidewalk, showing us some killer hackeysack tricks. In a funny way, he was a lot like Travis was on a skateboard, only there was no board, just a little bean bag. Tai did have a way of attracting a certain type.

Lenny was a scream. He was annoying the heck out of the Uptown crowd. Some giant guy in a three-piece Armani practically squashed Lenny, but Lenny managed to avoid the guy and cause him to bump smack into a guy even bigger, who was now threatening to go postal on the guy in the Armani. It was proving to be a way amusing lunch.

"What do you think of Lenny?" Tai asked. She

definitely got a blast out of her old pal, but at the same time she was way nervous that we might not approve of the whole picture.

Which we didn't. "It's not Lenny," I said. "He's really okay. And I swear, if he just bought himself a razor blade and learned how to use it, he could be a Baldwin."

"Yeah? Ya think so?" Tai asked.

"Definitely," I said. "But do you think hanging out with the hackeysack toast crew down in the village is the best thing for you, Tai?"

Tai shrugged. "I don't know. Lenny might be burnt around the edges, but he's a sweetheart," she said in his defense. "They all are."

"Sure, I know." Okay, I had to break it to her. "It's not that all your friends here aren't cool, Tai. But back in Beverly Hills, you were like way important. You really mattered. People were into you."

"The right people," De added.

"When we did that makeover, it really transformed you, Tai," I told her. "Remember how excellent it made you feel?"

Tai let out a long sigh. "I know you guys want the best for me and all. But it really is okay here. I mean, now that I live with my uncle and aunt, it's like they don't get all involved with my head. See, you guys won't know freedom until you split the Moms-and-Pops scene. Life without rules or curfews, it's totally cool, you know what I mean? I'm free as a bird, I can just come and go as I please."

"And fall asleep without getting out of your

clothes from the night before," I said. "Don't you feel all sticky after a while? I mean, seriously Tai, don't you miss doing the Betty thing?"

"Look, I know my attitude's a little yesterday."

"A little? Try a few weeks ago." I had to set her straight.

"Okay, but . . ." Tai was searching for words. "But—oh, I dunno."

"Look," I said. "At least admit that you miss Beverly Hills."

"Are you kidding, of course I miss it. I miss all that sunshine. And—"

"And Travis," I said. "Come on, you can say it. You're dying to see him."

"Yeah, sure I am," Tai said. "So how is he doing, anyway?"

De let out a long high-pitched whistle. "Forget it, Tai. Travis is in big trouble. Ever since you split, it's been a major nose dive for the guy. You'd barely recognize him, really."

"But he was so—evolved," she said. "And the Marvin the Martian skateboard I did for him, it was like leaving a piece of me there with him."

"Marvin's not enough. He needs all of you, girlfriend," De put in.

Great line. I could see Tai starting to crack a little.

"I don't know . . . yeah, I kind of wish we were still together, you know . . ." Tai had just gone from two-parts dazed to four-parts confused.

I put my hand on Tai's shoulder and motioned for

De to do the same. It felt like a total yearbook moment.

"Hey, I've got a great idea," I said. "What's the best way to get us all out of mood like this? And the number one answer is . . ."

"Shopping," Tai said, letting out a little bit of laughter. "Hey, come on, you didn't think I forgot *everything* you taught me, did you?"

"But unfortunately we lack major purchasing power," De reminded us.

"So we could put some stuff on hold," Tai said. "You know, lay-away. I do it all the time."

Sometimes that girl was *so* resourceful. I took a deep breath and readied myself for an all-out spree. "I already have it figured out," I told them. I'd memorized Christian's shopping route instructions from Bloomie's to Saks, with all the major stops in between.

With the hot dogs all finished, it was time for a major feast.

This was more like it. Especially for an up-and-coming fashion model. I had all the major designers on hold. A simply fabulous ice blue Chinese-style dress by Liza Bruce from Bloomingdale's, some way cool Prada cowhide boots at Barneys, these Jil Sander T-shirts—so righteously simple I'd had to take one in each color. At Bergdorf's I'd snagged several amazing suits—Dolce & Gabbana, Chanel, and this classic chocolate-colored pinstripe pants suit with a velvet collar by Andrea Jovine. And in between the biggies, those monster department stores crammed with all kinds of necessary items, we'd hit, oh, maybe several hundred little boutiques. Quick, efficient, professional.

We'd picked up most of the stuff on Christian's shopping list and found some golden souvenirs for everyone else back home. I wondered if Miss Mental Existential—M.E., as I was beginning to think of her—would like Josh in the silk Armani I had chosen for him. Not even. She probably had some song in her three-chord repertoire about exploited silkworms. But I refused to let them spoil my shopping trip. Besides, when I was on the cover of *Vogue*, Josh wouldn't be looking twice at her.

I had to add a few more outfits to my collection to get past the worries about my wayward boy. But I managed.

De didn't do badly herself. I think she was even starting to like New York. In the end, we had these impressively huge piles on hold at the counters of most of New York's finer stores. All we needed was the plastic from Daddy to take home our boxes and bags and bundles and more boxes.

Tai was impressed. "Whoa, you guys cleaned 'em out. Wow, I'd forgotten what umbuh-lievable shoppers you are. Lenny—aren't they, like, amazing?"

Lenny looked extra toasted. I guess the hackeysack wasn't enough to keep him in shape for the rigors of a major shopping spree. Tai looked a little tired, too. I knew she wasn't keeping up with the *Buns of Steel* tape we'd sent her home with. But she shook the sleepy look quick when De and I put the most adorable, special skirt and jacket on hold for her.

"A present," I told her. "You know, to deck you out Beverly Hills style again." All that shopping had really gotten me up. Some people get a runner's high. I go shopping.

"You guys!" Tai said, all happy and sad and stuff. "I miss you."

"Then come back," I said. "We miss you, too."

"Yeah, so what if your mom's strict," De said. "I'll bet she misses you big time, anyway."

Now Tai just looked plain old sad. "Well, she *has* been calling a lot." She swallowed hard.

"You miss her, too," I prodded. Tai was coming around. She had to be. By the end of the weekend, she'd be our own Tai again.

She shrugged and her eyes got all misty. The girl was a mess. Trashed. Torn up. She needed us. It was just so majorly unfair that we couldn't pay for her new outfit right away and get it on her before the show at Saks.

I had to settle for fiddling around with her hair in the Bendel's dressing room, and doing a number with the eye pencil and lipstick we'd snagged at Tai's. By then my trusty Movado said it was just about time for the big event.

I spiffed up my own do and freshened my makeup. I felt a shiver of nerves. What if this was my moment? What if Griffin's mistake about me was a sign—and I was about to be discovered? I had a truly weird flash: What if Tai belonged back in L.A., but I was destined to stay right here? Maybe fate had brought me east.

"Ready?" I asked De and Tai breathlessly.

But as we sailed out the Bendel's door, I experienced a sudden letdown. Something was wrong. I could just feel it. Or actually—not feel it. There was nothing in my arms. When had I ever left an important clothing store empty-handed?

I mean, sure, every other size six in New York City was being held for me right now, but after all that shopping, I didn't have a single new thing to wear to Griffin's show. Nothing. Nada. Not even one tiny well-placed accessory.

We stepped outside and I shivered. It was colder here, too. And as the afternoon turned into evening, the phrase "properly dressed" took on a complexity of meaning. A pair of sweat pants and a warm blanket wouldn't have been too shabby right now. A warm blanket—with Josh snuggling underneath.

All the shopping jollies fizzled away. Josh. What had I done? Here I was in the fashion capital of the world with no purchasing power, in the same tired outfit I'd been in for three thousand miles. Plus a few more to Brooklyn and back. While Josh was getting warm and fuzzy with *her*.

"Cher? Zup?" De asked.

I turned my palms up and shrugged. Boy, I usually couldn't do that after a package-laden bout of shopping. Then I spotted the street vendor who'd set up shop down the block, and it was like I smelled a good buy. I can't explain it. I just sort of know when there's something in the near vicinity that's worth taking home. It's a talent I have.

Without really even thinking about it, my feet were heading over there and I was inspecting his wares, and I was picking up these chronic—but I mean outrageously chic—pair of black thigh-highs, painted with a delicate white pattern up the outside of the leg. "How much?" I asked automatically.

The vendor held up the fingers on one hand. "Vedy goot price," he said. I was beginning to think that New York had seven million people, and just as many accents. "Hand-painted."

"Uh-huh? How about four bucks?" I asked. Even I had that. And would these go with my outfit, or what? They'd warm me up, too. Who needed Josh?

"Four-fifty, Miss," the vendor said.

I pretended that I was all like forget it, not even. I went as far as putting the thigh-highs back on the table and taking a few steps.

"Ole right, Miss. For you, four dollar."

I felt the shopping buzz return. Okay! "What do you think?" I asked De and Tai, picking up the stockings again.

De took a critical look. "Go, girl!" she approved.

"Cool!" Tai agreed.

I parted with my last Abraham Lincoln and got back a George. Down to my last dollar. But it was worth it. Now I could go to Griffin's show properly accessorized after all.

Chapter 11

*S*top right there! Perfect. Hold it. Come on, sweetie pie, let's see a little smile. Good." Flash. Pop. Snap, snap, snap. Griffin hadn't been exaggerating when he'd said this show was a big deal.

Saks was mobbed and the lights were bright. This was the place to be, and we were part of it. It was us and the beautiful people, the ones that mattered. Cameras clicking and flash bulbs popping nonstop. Just by walking in the door you'd rate at least a roll of film from one of the gazillions of photographers who were here. Billed as Saks Fifth Resort Wear— Here to Eternity, it was like The Event, and it was being recorded from every angle imaginable. This was the Kodak moment of the late twentieth century.

A photographer dressed head to toe in basic New

York black rushed up to us and started snapping away. First a group shot: De, Tai, Lenny, and me. Then he started to close in. I got prepared to dazzle him with my best Colgate. Face of the future, Cher Horowitz.

But then he was pointing his camera—and it was aimed right at Lenny! Lenny, like 501s-drooping-at-the-waist hadn't-shaved-in-two-weeks Lenny. I don't know, maybe the photographer was doing the arty thing, like capturing the down-and-out toast product mingling with the glitz. Either that or he thought Tai's wannabe boyfriend was some famous grunge rocker. Anyway, he kept snapping a whole bunch of close-ups, allowing Lenny to pretend he was the slacker of the moment.

"Umbuh-lievable. It's even wilder than on *The Real World*."

Sometimes Tai found just the right words to describe a situation. I wondered if she knew how big the smile was on her face right now. Or if she was thinking about how she wouldn't be here if it weren't for us. Tai had to see that things were just way more exciting with De and me. Thanks to us, even Lenny was in the spotlight.

I looked around and breathed in the energy. Seeing so many Alaïas, Versaces, and Chanels in one place sent my adrenaline into lunar orbit. And even for someone like me who came from Celeb Central, the guest list here was so totally impressive. I gave De a nudge when I spotted one of her all-time favorite actors sitting up front near the runway. "Check it out, De. There's—"

"Don't I know it, girlfriend. I spotted him the minute we got here. And how about over there, eleven o'clock." We were all "oh my god" at the sight of another paparazzi favorite amidst the crowd. "He looks even hotter in the flesh," De said. "And look, isn't he with what's-her-name? I thought she was married. That's *Hard Copy* material."

"Hey, guys. Over there. I swear I just saw him on 'Unplugged'!" Tai shouted. She was so dizzy she could barely stay on her feet. "Umbuh-lievable."

The crowd was one thing. All flash and fame and enough heady perfume to float Manhattan. But the stage was where the real action was. Supermodel after supermodel strutted down the runway, dazzling the audience in their outfits. The Here to Eternity theme was way happening, the stage done up with craters, stars, moon beams, and snorkel gear. It was a kind of other-planetary beach. Like imagine taking a two-week summer vacation on Pluto.

Kate, Naomi, Christy, Veronica—they were all there. And Cindy, too. Like I said, this was no small event. The stage was wall-to-wall Bettys. Not every-day babes. These were the kind that made regular Bettys seem more like Monets. I couldn't believe that I was thinking I could compete with people like Cindy. Her dot alone did me in.

And then, just when I thought my fashion career

had ended before it ever started, this guy was handing me a curve-tracing maillot swimsuit and a sheer chiffony coverup. "Better hurry up," he said. "You've got two minutes to runway time."

The runway? *Moi?* I was shocked into silence. I stared at the not-yet-in-the-stores confection in my arms as the guy who'd handed me the outfit disappeared backstage. I guess we were standing a little too close to the dressing-room doorway, or something.

Major gulp. Talk about getting catapulted into the spotlight. Like now what do I do? Answer—break out in a rash.

De looked even more surprised than I was. I'd never seen a pair of eyes open up so wide. "Here's your big chance, girlfriend," she said. "You're on in two."

My eyes fixed on the runway and on Cindy's dot. Me, up there? With them? I was frozen stiff.

"So I wasn't the only one who mistook you for a cover girl."

I turned around and saw Griffin. Whoa, did things happen fast in New York. I could feel my heart flutter a total schoolgirl beat as I looked at Griffin. Dazzling blue eyes, killer smile. One look and I was thawing fast.

"Come on, Cher, it'll be a blast," he said with a wink.

"Are you serious? I mean—"

"Hey, you're a killer, Cher. It's breaks like these

that people die for. It'll be fun, and I'll be on the stage right next to you, so there's nothing to worry about. Trust me."

I glanced back up at the stage and then back at the outfit. Kamali. I was terrified. "I don't know. I mean, Kamali? It's just not me. Cut's all wrong for my shape . . ."

"Cher, are you mentally challenged?" Dionne asked.

And as I stood there flipping, another designer's assistant appeared and simply whisked the Kamali out of my hands. "Who are you?" he sniffed, giving me the old once-over. "And how did you get that? Willow's supposed to be on in that right now."

"Wait!" I called after him, suddenly ready to make my modeling debut, after all. But it was too late.

Griffin gave me a little pat. "Hey, don't sweat it, Cher. No reason to make your first appearance in the wrong outfit. Trust your instincts. You're going to go far," he assured me.

"I am?" I asked, still holding my arm out to the vanished Kamali.

"Sure. I gotta get to work, now, but wait for me after the show, I'll have time to introduce you to some of the big hitters, okay?"

"Well, um, definitely okay," I managed. "See you then," I added.

Except between now and then, I got to see him at least a half dozen times, heading down the runway in clothes that ranged from sublime and sensational to just plain silly. A pair of perfectly cut linen drawstring pants—*très* sexy *sans* shirt and shoes. A nonsensical turn-of-the-century-style swimsuit that looked like a sleeveless unitard. Still, Griffin looked awesome in everything.

Wow! He was the kind of guy you could leave your husband and children for. The kind of guy you could leave your—Josh? This New York thing definitely had a way of making you forget sometimes. Griffin? What was I thinking? I didn't even know his last name!

And then I remembered how many rings I'd waited through the last time I'd tried calling Josh. Had I tried him three, or was it four, times since leaving Beverly Hills? Like if you give the guy you love your cellular, isn't he supposed to wear it always? And answer it when you call?

So I let myself forget about him for a while and enjoyed the fantasy as I checked out Griffin onstage. The next thing I knew, I felt someone's hands all over my legs. I looked down, and there was this weird woman on her knees, desperately trying to take my thigh-highs off!

"Where *did* you get these?" she said, still on all fours, tugging at me. She had a loud whiny voice. "These leggings are precious. I need them!" she shrieked.

"Huh? Like, hello down there, would you mind getting off my legs!" I stepped away, trying to protect myself from this wacko.

"Don't you know who I am?" she asked as she

rose to her feet. She sounded one part shocked, two parts annoyed.

Okay, so I didn't recognize her. I mean I did know tons about the wonderful world of fashion, but you couldn't hold me accountable for every single face.

The woman looked nervously at her watch, like she had a plane to catch or something. "Look, dearie, I really don't have time to play games. My girls go on in exactly three and a half minutes. I'm inspired, and when I'm inspired I get what I need. I want your stockings, and I want them now. Consider it a compliment that somebody like me likes your style. Now let's do business."

This day was getting weirder and weirder. New York was a little like a series of episodes from *Tales from the Dark Side*.

"Whatever you paid for them, I'll double it," the woman said as she reached into her slacks pocket for cash.

I thought about the guy right outside Saks selling these thigh-highs for pocket change. I also thought about how Daddy's money had yet to arrive. If this clothes vulture wanted to pay me to rip the socks off my legs, who was I to stop her. "Well, okay, I guess I don't have any choice but to part with them. I paid four—yeah, for-ty dollars."

The woman didn't even blink. She peeled off four crisp twenties and I peeled off the thigh-highs and handed them to her. I tucked the money safely into you-know-where. De and I slapped each other a subtle five. I did the quick calculation in my head and realized I'd made a two-thousand-percent prof-it. Daddy would have been so proud.

Maybe it was the glow of newfound wealth. I'd had money. I'd lost it. Now I had it again. At least enough to carry me through the next few hours, until Daddy came through with the real goods. I think the confidence of crisp bills showed. After bumming at blowing my chance at walking the runway, I felt like I had regained that old je ne sais quoi. That's French for I was bathing in some righteous vibes. I could almost feel the packages in my arms and the drape of brand-new, well-cut silks and linens on my body.

Whatever it was, Griffin must have seen it on me. He just kind of parted the after-the-show crowd that had gathered around him, and we came together as if it were totally natural. "Hey, baby," he said, giving me a kiss on the cheek.

Pop! I wasn't sure whether I was more startled by the flash of the camera capturing the moment or the distinct smell and feel of Griffin's lipstick on my face. Lipstick? Wait a sec. . . . Then I reminded myself that it was just a tool of the trade.

"How'd you like the show?" he asked.

"It was—"

"People said I looked really good up there," he added, before I'd gotten a complete answer out of my mouth.

"Oh, yeah, totally," I said. "You were—big-time decent."

"Thanks, Cher." He put an arm around me. Suddenly I caught De and Tai looking at us, and I felt a little uncomfortable. The kiss, his arm around me. I kind of eased away from him.

He frowned. "Hey, listen," he said, leaning close in again, "I want you to meet my agent. Christianne!" A tall, severe-looking brunette turned around.

Griffin's agent! I put on my most Colgate smile, and this time I didn't resist the hold of his lean well-muscled arm. Christianne was probably in her midforties but dressed in her midtwenties—top shelf labels from head to toe. "Griffin, darling," she said. She didn't even look at me.

"Hey, Christianne. Good show, huh? Listen, this is my new friend, Cher." He gave me a little squeeze.

"Nice to meet you," Christianne said automatically. My je ne sais quoi did a little nose dive.

"So! What do you think?" Griffin persisted.

"Yes, of course, darling. Good show. *Fabulous* show."

"No, I mean Cher."

"Oh." Christianne studied me coolly. I felt like it said "clueless" right across my forehead. "Hmm. Fresh-looking," she said. Oh. Did that mean I wasn't a hopeless case? "Do something about that nose, shape the eyebrows and the hair a bit—not bad. How tall are you, dear? Five six?"

"Five seven."

"Oh, well, maybe another inch or two would do it."

And then she and Griffin were air-kissing, and before I knew what was happening, she was gone. So much for that glow I'd gotten along with the four twenties.

"See? I told you these folks would love you," Griffin said.

"Please." I sniffled. "She said I was too short and my eyebrows were wrong and that my nose . . ." I shook my head. In a school where nose jobs are the number one topic for "What I Did on My Christmas Vacation," I'd always been sort of proud of my au naturel.

"Oh, a nip here, a tuck there. No biggie. It takes most of us a lot more than that."

"It does?" I found myself looking at Griffin and wondering what parts of him were plastic. The perfect bone structure? The sexy, pouty mouth? What about those incredible baby blues? Then he showered me with a smile, and I nearly forgot about everything. Including his lipstick. Listen, the guy was like a top-ten Baldwin. No two ways about it. And he had me pegged for a Betty.

"Here, Cher, smile for the cameras," he was saying. He put his face close to mine. "The cameras love you, everyone loves you. That's the most important thing."

It made sense. So I turned the smile back on. And as the flashes went off, I started to feel better again. Here I was, being photographed along with Griffin— and Cindy and all the other stellar lights in the room.

"Who is she?" I heard someone nearby ask, and I

knew she was wondering about me. Cher Horowitz. Well, okay, just Cher. Some of the brightest don't need more than one name.

And then Griffin was bussing me right on the mouth, and the cameras were going wild. I drank in his kiss and the attention of the crowd.

"Okay, baby, so I'll see you at the post-show party? Everyone's going to the Fashion Café," he whispered in my ear.

"And what about now?" I was still stunned by the kiss.

"Oh. Gotta get out of these threads. Wash up. But I'll meet you later. Promise. Here. I've got three extra invites. Private party and all."

I took the tickets he dug out of his pocket. "The Fashion Café. That's the place owned by—"

"Elle. And Naomi and Christy and Claudia," said Griffin. "See and be seen. Name of the game. And you'll be the new dish on the menu, Cher. See you there?" he asked.

Then he was Audi. Swallowed by the up-to-the-moment crowd. I wasn't sure what to think. No way you'd ever hear Josh recommending a few nips and tucks. But no way hanging out with Josh was going to set off any paparazzi cameras, either.

Well, one thing was for sure. I wasn't going to miss the scene at the Fashion Café. I wiped off Griffin's lipstick and headed over to tell De and Tai that we had three tickets to the hottest party in New York City.

Chapter 12

I shop, therefore I am. Especially in a place like New York City. If Josh wanted me to take a more philosophical approach, there it was. I got myself a decent lipstick before we even left Saks. Then I replaced the thigh-highs. Well, actually, I bought two more pairs. Then, joy of joys, we found a guy selling all kinds of home electronics out of some boxes he'd set up on the street. Answering machines, calculators—and yes, phones, including that basic necessity, the cellular. Unfortunately, all he had was this unpleasant yellowy beige. Didn't match anything I had on, but it would have to do in a pinch. No more New York pay phones or hand dialing. I had to spend most of my profit from that fashion lady, but hey—I was wired again, so it was worth it.

We wound up spending the rest of it on skim mochaccinos. Not that I needed a pick-me-up. I was still on a high-octane buzz from the fashion show. So many things had happened today, I felt like I'd probably never return to planet earth. But as the New York sky went from daytime gray to dark gray, De and Tai were struggling to keep their lids open. And forget about Lenny. He was out solid, his head a dead weight on Tai's shoulder.

"Come on already, answer," I said to my new cellular.

But it didn't seem to matter what phone I tried Josh from; he wasn't picking up on the California end. I let it ring one hundred or so times, trying not to let thoughts of Josh and that Mental, Mental girl get me buggin'.

"Maybe his cel is dead and he hasn't figured it out yet. It's not like Josh has a clue about machines. Or maybe he just plain lost it," De suggested. "Besides, isn't Josh sort of history? Or are you two-timing now?"

That was way harsh. And undeserved, too. I mean that little kiss between Griffin and me didn't mean a thing. And it happened so fast, I didn't even have a chance to judge quality.

No, De had it all wrong for sure. That kiss was just for the cameras, wasn't it? A kiss and a smile—it was model stuff, like so the toothpaste companies knew you had teeth, just in case they were looking for a new set of pearly whites to promote their product. Griffin was showing me how to establish the right image for the public. Like Michael and Lisa Marie. They didn't really expect us to believe they were for real.

I put down the cellular and picked up my teaspoon to stir the coffee. Flash. I saw my reflection in the silver of the spoon. For an all-too-brief moment I saw myself as Cindy, minus the dot. There I was, the discovery of the minute—famous, exquisite, near perfect. I was the "it" girl. Only when I looked a little closer, it was like, who's the Monet? Even in the tiny little spoon, the flaws were there.

Start with a nose that was somehow wrong. And eyebrows that needed serious help. Thin hair, a zit about to happen on my chin. And that was just in the spoon. There was the height problem, too. I mean, did I have to get some plastic doctor to give me a permanent heel lift, too? Where did you draw the line, anyway?

Tai was all "Cher, what are you doing?"

"Huh?" She'd caught me smiling at a spoon. Okay, so I was making sure my teeth were white enough for Colgate. The supermodel life was rough. It was like every second you were getting pinched and pricked, tested and corrected. And then when you thought you had it all together, the fashion would change and you'd need to get recorrected. And it didn't matter what you really looked like, it mattered what you looked like to the camera.

From way out in left field, Lenny picked his head up off of Tai's shoulder and dropped onto the table. Then he started snoring, right there in the cafe. He was so loud the guys sitting next to us got up and moved to a different table.

"Does he do this often?" I asked.

Tai was way embarrassed. "Once in a while, yeah. But he's really okay," she insisted.

"Hey, I like him," De said. "Really. It's just that—"

"I know," Tai said. "He's sort of on the toasty side. Yeah, I know I could do a lot better."

"You already did do a lot better. Remember Travis?" I asked. "Don't you miss him?"

"You know I do," Tai said, turning instantly dreamy. "No one ever loved my Marvin comics as much as Travis. And man, did he kiss great! You know, like just enough mouth but not too wet."

De and I flashed each other the whatever sign. I was dying to get Tai back with us, but did we have to get the lowdown on Travis Birkenstock's lips? "So what do you say, Tai. Are you coming back to Beverly Hills where you belong?"

Tai gave her usual long sigh, accompanied by a shrug that was more a slump. "I don't know. I'm like this yo-yo with a three-thousand-mile string. I can't figure out what to do. I mean, I really do miss him and all, but—"

"Hey, maybe if you talk to him you'll see how much you guys need each other," De suggested.

"Great idea," I said as I handed the beige phone to Tai. "Dial."

She hesitated, then started punching Travis's number. She still knew it by heart. I could tell she was nervous, and she wasn't sure if she was relieved or bummed when she got his answering machine.

"The message says he's not home and even if he was he wouldn't answer because life stinks," Tai said as she clicked off and handed me the phone. "Wow, he didn't sound so good. You guys think it's because of me?"

"Duh! Hel-lo! Come in, Tai. Of course it's you."

"Don't you get it, girl?" De said. "Travis needs you back in his life."

"And I've got news for you—your mom does, too," I reminded her.

"If I go back, my mom will probably make me stay in the house forever. For all I know, she won't even let me go out to go to school. I'll have to do one of those correspondence programs."

"I thought you didn't even have a VCR," I said.

"Oh, yeah," Tai said. "Wow, life's just so hard to figure out. What am I going to do?"

"What are any of us going to do?" I asked. Okay, so now I was getting way philosophical. I don't know, maybe it was the coffee-bar atmosphere. Call me a sap, but the place kind of reminded me a lot of Josh. It was filled with all these unshaven college-age guys getting a buzz on caffeine and complaint rock. I felt way out of place, which was always how I felt around Josh and his crowd. I really missed him.

But it was De who grabbed the phone and started dialing. "You guys are getting too heavy on me. I think I need to get back in touch with the real world. I'm calling Murray, just to hear his voice. And if he doesn't pick a fight with me within two minutes, then I'll know something's wrong and I'll be joining you two in the land of the lost."

No sooner had De said, "Hi, Murray," then the fireworks began.

"Hold on one cross-continental minute!" De shouted into the phone. "If I told you once, I told you a thousand times, cut the 'woman' rap, do you hear me, homie? I don't like it in Beverly Hills, and I don't like it in New York. And don't think I don't know you're Jeepin' with Yolanda even as we speak. I hear her mousy little two-timing voice in the background. I don't care if she's your cousin, that girl is no friend of mine!" De hung up in a huff. "That boy just makes my heart flutter something awful."

At least someone had a solid relationship. You could tell by De's wall-to-wall smile that Murray was all hers.

Tai was smiling, too. Maybe she was remembering Travis's lips. Whatever it was, I was getting the feeling that she was seeing things a lot more clearly now. I was almost sure that she'd be taking that flight back to Beverly Hills.

What I wasn't sure about was me. It was like my fate still needed to be determined. Well, we had those three tickets to the party at the Fashion Café. Sorry, Lenny, but you're the odd man out. It was time to find Griffin and see what was in my future.

* * *

As we were paying our java bill, my cellular phone rang. No time wasted between my very recent call to the hotel to leave them my new mobile number and the sweet chiming of my Alexander Graham Bell. Oh, that ring! I loved my way ugly new phone. It felt like old times again.

"Josh! I knew he'd call!" I said as I clicked the phone on. "Josh? Sweetie? I miss you."

"What do you mean 'Josh'?" came the angry, gruff voice. It was Daddy. And it sounded like Daddy after a really bad day at the office. "No, Cher, I'm sorry to disappoint you, but this is your father. Remember me? I'm the one who saw you through diapers, braces, and training bras. Your father, Cher. That slightly overweight middle-age guy with the wallet who has always made it possible for you to live life to its fullest."

"About that wallet, Daddy. I just called the hotel, and we still haven't got the money you wired. What happened?"

"How do I know what happened?" He was not sounding good. He definitely needed some t.l.c. from his one and only.

"Daddy, chill, okay. Take a few deep breaths and try to calm yourself. Remember that relaxation tape I got for you? Maybe you should listen to it, now."

"Never mind the baloney, Cher, just tell me when you're coming home."

"My flight is for tomorrow afternoon, but—"

"But? What but?" he said, sounding extra exasperated. "If your flight is tomorrow, then you'll be home tomorrow."

Maybe it wasn't the best time to bring up my potential modeling career. I mean, I wasn't even sure what was happening myself, yet. "I just meant that De and I were still working on our friend, Tai. Remember? I just might have to stay another day or—"

"Tai schmai, I want you home, do you understand me?"

Even with my lifelong lessons from Daddy in the art of arguing, I wasn't sure how I was going to get around this one. "I'll be home Monday at the latest, okay?"

"Cher, you know I'm not a patient man!" Daddy shouted.

"Is everything okay at home, Daddy?" I asked, trying my best to change the subject.

"No, Cher. Everything at home stinks," Daddy said. "I woke up this morning, and it seemed like a normal day. Only then I remembered that my daughter—my only daughter—was in New York City of all places, with no money and no clue. And then some strange lady who doesn't even speak English tried to get me to drink some awful green concoction."

"That's Lucy. She's our housekeeper," I told him. "And you're supposed to drink your vegetable juice every morning. Remember, your cholesterol level was pushing two-fifty."

"Cher, listen to me," Daddy pleaded. "I can't find

my blue linen shirt, my socks don't match, I've got horrible indigestion. I'm lost in my own house, Cher. I need you back here."

I figured it would be better not to press any harder on the issue of my staying in New York and pursuing a modeling career. "I'll be home soon, Daddy. Just drink your juice and take your cholesterol medicine like a good boy, and everything will be okay."

"Everything won't be okay until I see you back here, safe and sound, Cher."

"I'll be home soon, Daddy. And don't worry, I'll find all your things, and don't forget I'm going to bring you black and whites."

"Just another reason you are going to hurry right home, young lady!"

Chapter 13

*I*t looked like the runway shoot had just been an excuse for the real party. Fashion Café was The Place. Outside the restaurant, the taxis and limos were causing a traffic jam. A crowd of wanna-enters bloomed around the door. The honking cars sounded like party horns to me.

It was way cool to breeze on in like we were already somebodies on the New York scene. "Yo, I saw them on Page Six," I heard one of the doorway gawkers saying as they let us through the crowd.

I wasn't sure what this Page Six was, but I figured the guy had laid a compliment on us. I did my best to look as if I came to these kinds of events every night. I wished some of the gang back in Beverly Hills could see us making our way into the spacious restaurant, the band playing, the food and drinks flowing. I especially wished big-haired, big-mouthed Amber could see us. She was always bragging about all the movie stars she'd powwowed with in Hollyrock. Not that any of us believed her. But at this party, the stars were real. Well, some of them, at least.

"Check it out! Kate Moss!" De exclaimed as we took a table with a good view. There, in a private corner, stood Kate Moss with a few friends. Wait. No, she just looked like Kate Moss.

"Not even," I told De. "Oh, wow, but *there's* Kate coming in through the door with—no. Never mind." She was a look-alike, too.

Whatever. There were plenty of genuine articles. The very real, very golden Naomi Campbell was playing hostess in a Josie Natori halter and long skirt, greeting people as they came in. Veronica Webb was table-hopping in Marc Jacobs. I figured the true Kate Moss would show up eventually. Maybe with the most brutal Baldwin of the late twentieth century— her boyfriend, Johnny Depp.

The three of us—me, Tai, and Dionne— stargazed as we loaded up at the buffet table. Well, Tai loaded up, sampling a little of everything. Dionne went for the elegantly moderate—smoked salmon, side of pasta, and vegetables. One piece of caviar on toast, because it was a special occasion. I looked at the banquet hungrily. I'd worked up an appetite on our shopping marathon. But I forced myself to dine on carrot sticks and celery. Phat was one thing. Fat was completely another. Especially for an up-and-coming model.

"Ooh, isn't that guy like some famous rock star?" Tai asked as she made her way back to our table balancing her heavy plate.

I followed her gaze. A sort of older dude with a mane of long blond curls and a skintight pair of leather pants was drinking champagne with a pretty blonde.

"Rachel Hunter!" I said in awe. "So he must be—"

"Rod Stewart!" De finished. "Yeah, wow! I know about him. My mom saw him in concert back in the old days like the seventies or eighties or something."

We played a hearty game of Name That Face as we ate dinner. Or, rather, as I did up the no-cal crunchies and Tai and De put away the mouth-watering meal. It helped a little to see all these Betty types doing the carrot munch, too.

Suddenly, there was this smooth voice at my ear, going, "Hey, you lovely California girls having fun?"

"Griffin!" Be still, my beating heart. He looked hotter than ever, all scrubbed and naked-faced, in a pair of perfectly fitting jeans and a plain T-shirt. He pulled up a chair.

"So? Nice party?"

"Totally!" I exclaimed. "Do you hang with all these cover models all the time?"

Griffin shrugged—like no biggie.

"Mmm, this is, like, way happening," Tai said. But then she let out this huge yawn.

"That good, huh?" Griffin asked.

I was embarrassed. Like what if Griffin thought we were out past our bedtime?

Tai laughed. "No, really. I mean, this is like incredible and stuff. But you know—long day, good meal. I could go for forty winks." She stretched her arms in the air, all sleepy.

"Tai, I thought you came back to New York so you could stay out all night," I said.

"Yeah." She shrugged. "Maybe it wasn't such a good idea."

De kicked me under the table. "That's what we've been trying to tell you, Tai."

"Well, maybe you were right."

For a second, the scene around me kind of went away. "Does that mean you're ready to come home?" I asked.

Tai blew out a long breath. "Well, Travis evolved, right? And my mother evolved. I mean, okay, the new responsible her is sort of like the Great Dictator of the mom world. But I've been thinking . . . maybe I need to evolve, too. Leave the old Tai and my old life behind."

I let out a jubilant "Yes!"

"I mean, my New York is so—so yesterday compared to this. And to L.A. And anyway, it's no fun staying out all night without Travis and you guys. Especially Travis."

"So you're coming home?" I asked.

Tai gave me a sheepish smile and nodded. "Besides, okay, like I'll admit it. My mom misses me. I miss her. Maybe we can work things out."

Mission accomplished! De and I exchanged high-fives, low-fives, and our special Beverly Hills limp-wrist miss. I just love a happy ending.

"Welcome home, girlfriend," De said. We all hugged each other.

And then I was just so jubilant that I hugged Griffin, too. And I felt his broad shoulders under his T-shirt, his hold was strong and sure, and his face was really close to mine and—

"Ahem!" Tai was saying. "Um, like, I'm glad everyone's glad, but I'm still really tired, so I think I'm gonna take off."

I looked over at her and De without letting go of Griffin. De was staring at the two of us, sizing us up. "Yeah, well. I guess I'm Audi, too," she said pointedly.

"Cher, you're not going, are you?" I felt the tickle of Griffin's breath on my cheek as he spoke. "Mizrahi hasn't even arrived yet. Calvin, either."

Calvin? The scene at the restaurant came zooming on back in focus. When would I ever have this kind of chance again? "No, I'm not going," I answered Griffin. "You guys go ahead," I added to Tai and De.

De raised an eyebrow. Perfectly arched, by the way. "You sure you'll be okay? You don't want to hang back at the hotel?"

"Tscha!" I snuggled closer to Griffin. Everyone who was anyone in the fashion world was here. Or on the way. Let De and Tai snag the old Zzzs. This was going to be my moment.

The cameras continued to pop, and I tried hard to show only my good side. Without De and Tai to remind me that they knew me when, I could really get into acting the part of the fashion-model-to-be. I matched Griffin, smile for smile. It was tough work. After a while my face hurt, and I thought my jaw was going to get locked for life. I could see now why there were so many face lifts in the business. Smiling twenty-four hours a day put your face in serious wrinkle jeopardy.

I held on to Griffin's arm as he led me around the Fashion Café like I was his prima ballerina. Not only was he a Baldwin with strong arms, he was Mr. Cool and Casual. He could say, "Hi, you look fab," to a half-dozen people at once, and he knew exactly where the cameras were and who was important enough to exchange an air kiss with.

"You'll have it all down fast," he assured me. "It just takes practice." He put his hand to his lips and threw a juicy one clear across the room.

"Who was that for?" I asked.

"Cindy. Come on, I'll introduce you."

Gulp. I was ready to audition, but I didn't think I was that ready. I wondered if Radu was going to be with her.

I tried not to tremble as we made our way through the thick crowd. Get it together, Cher, I told myself. She was just a person. With a dot.

But by the time we got there, the crowd was so thick around her that Griffin decided we'd wait until later. "You never want to seem desperate, Cher," he said. "Come on, let's sit for a minute."

He led me to a two-seater couch that was kind of tucked away from the rest of the place. Here we were in the middle of the brightest, most crowded place in New York, and Griffin had somehow managed to find the one spot that was dark and deserted. Up till then he'd been way smooth. But as he pulled me close and nuzzled my neck, he was exposing me to his other side—the one that was one hundred percent male beast, in a rush, and totally obvious about it.

Not yet, Griffin. I wriggled free. "What about all those people out there. Remember, you were going to introduce me?"

"Oh, yeah, right, that," he mumbled.

That? It was only my whole career. Well, if he needed a little coaxing, then coaxing was what he was going to get. I gave him a way friendly squeeze, right on the back of his neck, and ran my fingers through his long smooth hair. Actually, it felt nice. But we had work to do, people to meet.

"Okay," he said. He got up and took my hand. "Let's see who we can find."

Griffin knew everybody. So it took about a half second to locate Fashion Expert Number One.

"This guy's amazing," Griffin said as he introduced me to Manolo. "Meet my new hot friend,

Cher, from L.A. Her dad's a big-time movie exec on the coast."

Movie exec? The last time Daddy had anything to with Hollywood was when he sued Disney. Oh! That comment I'd made about Daddy working with people in the film business—Griffin had taken it totally the wrong way. But I was in no position to correct him. My career was in the making.

Manolo was a photographer whose specialty was close-ups. He did faces, hair, eyes—those very Revlon parts. So when he leaned in so close that I could smell the Listerine, I knew I was being given the major once-over by an expert.

Manolo held my chin firmly with his thumb and index finger and moved my face around in every direction. "Uh-huh. Uh-huh. Nice. Yes. No. No."

I wondered if he knew any two- or three-syllable words.

He pressed his fingers firmly into my jaw. "She didn't have her back molars removed yet?" he asked, sounding surprised.

I looked at Griffin for an explanation.

"To define your cheek bones," he said, quite matter-of-factly. "It's a must, Cher. No biggie."

"That's because they're not your molars! Thank you very much, I think I'll keep mine."

Manolo looked at me like I was totally clueless. "Send me your head shots after the teeth get removed. I might be able to work with you, Cher. Oh, and do something about that freckle," he said.

How could he even see it? I had this tiny freckle on the side of my face that was only a tiny shade darker than the rest of my skin. It didn't even show up on my computer scanner. "I have to have that removed, too?" I asked.

"No, no," Manolo said, shaking his head in frustration. "Darker. Make it darker. It may be just what you need."

Manolo flitted off into the crowd, lost in the sea of beauty. Meanwhile, I couldn't keep my tongue from exploring the back portion of my mouth, going over each molar as if for the last time. I doubted my dentist in Beverly Hills was going to approve of messing with my corrected bite.

"Griffin, you gorgeous hunk!" came a shout from behind us. This rail-thin, thirty-something brunette, caked to the limit with makeup, wrapped her arms around Griffin. "Where have you been hiding, Romeo?"

Griffin flashed her his famous life's-the-best smile and pressed his cheek against hers for a moment. "Roxy, babe, I missed you."

I couldn't quite figure out who Roxy was. She might have been a model once. Like a generation and a half ago. Under the bright lights of the Fashion Café, the three-layer makeup job couldn't hide the fact that this thirty-something Roxy was really pushing fifty.

"Roxy, I want you to meet Cher. You don't know her yet because she's been hiding out in a little ghost town in Nebraska all her life," Griffin said as he twirled me around for a total display.

Nebraska? So now he was peddling me as the farmer's-daughter type.

"Roxy is a talent scout for one of the biggies," Griffin said. "Isn't she something, Roxy?"

"She's something else," Roxy said with a pair of eyebrows that rose so high they almost fell right off her face.

So much for working for Roxy's company. According to her, I was too young for *Cosmo* and too old for *Seventeen.* "But wait a minute," she said as she grabbed my left hand and brought it up to her face. "Yes, I think we have something here. These hands are precious. I could call the Palmolive people and set up a test shoot."

I had an instant vision of wrapping up my "What I Did in New York" story with "and then I was soaking my hands in dishwashing liquid . . ."

"Have her call me, Griffin, honey. We'll set up an appointment for next Tuesday. Wednesday at the latest." And then she was Audi as she spotted yet another fabulous hunk at the buffet table.

"Was she serious?" I asked Griffin.

Griffin took my hands in his and put them to his lips. "About your hands? They are precious, Cher."

"Thanks a lot," I said as I pulled them away.

"Hey, wait a minute. Don't forget I'm the one who spotted you in the first place. You're a knockout, Cher, believe me."

"Really?" I felt my spirits rising. Griffin did have a way of making a girl feel special.

"Really. Hey, Roxy's had a few too many, anyway. But if we can get you in her office for a go-see, she'll realize then that you're A-list material."

"Maybe, but I'm not going to give up my life in Beverly Hills if all I'm going to be is a pair of hands. Might as well cut them off and send the rest of me back home to Nebraska."

"Hey, that was just business stuff," Griffin said. "Sometimes you've got to tell them what you think they want to hear."

The party was getting more packed by the minute. "Don't give up, yet, Cher," Griffin said. He gave me a hug. "There's always somebody else who can make you a star. That's what's so great about New York."

And sure enough, the second we stopped hugging, there was Jean-Luc in a skintight black jumpsuit and a pair of late disco-look gummy stack heels. With the six-inch heels, Jean-Luc maybe came up to my chin.

"Big-time video director. And he owes me a huge favor," Griffin whispered to me.

I smiled, wondering how this tiny little man was going to help launch my career.

"Jean-Luc, remember my dear friend, Cher? She just got back from a three-month shoot in Italy. You've heard of her, of course," Griffin said, sounding totally believable.

Jean-Luc nodded. "All I'm interested een is wezer

she can dence," he said as he gave me the once-over. "I'm zhooting a heaby metal veedeeo next week. I need dencers. So, like I say, eef you can dence, I can use you."

Griffin gave my hand an encouraging squeeze. "See, I told you that your time was here."

"Count me in!" I heard myself saying.

And then Jean-Luc dumped the whole story on me. He looked me in the eye and told me one hundred percent seriously that I'd need to shave my head and tattoo my scalp. "For ze zake of ze art," he explained.

My head went from spinning to spun. I tried to make a polite exit to the little girls' room.

As I stood in front of the bathroom mirror, I started adding up all the criticism. Let's see, if I started with molar removal and ended with a tattooed head, and in between I fixed my nose, redid my hair, grew two inches, and did who-knows-what to my eyes, I just might have what it took to be a someone.

It did occur to me that with a shaved head to star in a video, I could still use my hands for the dishwashing liquid shoot. Maybe I did have something after all.

As if. What I needed was a reminder that the unaltered Cher was enough. I mean, my beloved mother died during liposuction. Beauty is so important, but it does have its limits. Plastic is for lawn chairs. If anyone could assure me of that, it was Josh.

I started dialing, willing him to answer, say he loved me and beg me to come home on the next plane. Thirty rings later there was still no Josh. Mental, Mental, Existential.

I found Griffin waiting for me back at the party and practically fell right into his waiting arms. "Next stop?" I asked.

Griffin nuzzled my neck, and I decided to enjoy it this time. "It's your call, Cher."

"How about someplace where the people are a little nicer. I don't want anybody else suggesting I change body parts."

"Maybe we should head downtown. The crowd's a lot more accepting," Griffin said. "And there'll be people to meet there, too. This magazine editor I know . . . have you ever been to a poetry slam?"

I shook my head. " 'Will there really be a "Morning"? Is there such a thing as "Day"? Could I see it from the mountains if I were as tall as they?' "

"Huh? Hey, Cher, you gotta stop worrying about being a little short."

"It's a poem," I said. "Emily Dickinson." I was too mad at Josh to even give him credit for teaching me that one. "Let's do the slam," I said. I held on to Griffin's strong arm as he led us out past the Naomis and the Christys and the Cindys. I turned and blew a final air kiss to them all, wondering if I'd ever be back.

Chapter 14

*T*hey were both going too fast—the taxi driver and Griffin.

The cabbie was doing this solo drag-racing thing right down a narrow street that still managed to have traffic on it in the small hours of the morning. He squealed around the right side of a delivery truck and then peeled left around another cab. He added a few honks and swore in some foreign tongue. Well, you didn't need a driver's license in New York. At least it didn't seem that way—and that was good news for me.

Griffin didn't appear to notice that our lives were in danger. He tickled my ear with his lips and kissed my cheek. "You're as beautiful as any of those cover girls," he whispered.

"I am?" I was flattered. One person thought I had star potential.

"Sure," Griffin said easily. The taxi took another sharpie and I was jolted just about into his lap.

"Mmm, I love it when you throw yourself at me," he murmured, wrapping his arms around me and keeping us pressed together.

I laughed nervously. Don't get me wrong. Griffin was hunk city. Babe-a-licious. His arms felt way excellent around me. Plus, he really thought I could get behind the camera with the best of them. That alone made my heart bump and thump faster. That and the wild ride.

But you've got to understand something: In some ways, I'm really an old-fashioned girl. Griffin was all go for it now and stuff. And part of me wanted to. But look—I'd known Josh for years before we even said anything nice to each other. And Griffin had a lot more in mind than just saying a few things.

The taxi driver floored it on a relatively empty stretch. Griffin's hands went exploring.

Brring! My phone! Saved by the bell! I grabbed it off the taxi seat where it lay next to me. "Hello?" My heart raced. Maybe it was Josh.

"Cher. Where *are* you? Sounds like you're out playing in traffic in the middle of the night."

"Daddy—again?" I asked.

"And, by the way, there's no sugar for the coffee, and that woman—what's her name? I can't find her anywhere."

"Her name is Lucy, Daddy, and she's off on

Saturday. And anyway, you shouldn't be having coffee at—what time is it there? Midnight? Especially not with sugar. There's some nice chamomile tea over the dishwasher."

"And?" Daddy growled.

"And what? Oh, there's a honey bear up there, too."

"You know what I mean, Cher. And just exactly where is my sixteen-year-old daughter, right this second?"

"Well . . . where do you think I should be?" I asked, shooting a sideways glance at Griffin.

"I think you should be asleep."

"How can I be, Daddy, when you're calling me up in the middle of the night?"

"Cher, do you mean to tell me that you and your mobile phone are safe and sound in your hotel room? What are all those car horns?"

"Oh, Daddy, there's just a lot of noise in the street," I said. That much was true. "You don't remember how noisy New York is."

All of a sudden, there's this crackle over the phone and some strange voice is going, "Car thirty-seven. Come in thirty-seven. Pick up at thirty-third and third . . ."

And Daddy's all "Cher? Cher, who is that?"

And Griffin's kind of talking to himself and he's like "Daddy! She's on the phone with her father!"

And the cabbie's cursing out some other driver in a language with lots of S's and Z's.

"Look, Daddy, we have a totally bad connection,"

I said. "I'm fine. I promise. Now, don't worry. I'll call you tomorrow." I got off before I had to tell a real lie.

"Chamomile tea?" Griffin asked.

"Oh, yeah. It's seriously good for relaxing," I told him.

"I know something else that's good for relaxing," he said. And then he was taking away my phone and stashing it in his bag. "No more interruptions," he said. "Now, where were we?" And his mouth went in for a landing on my neck.

Inside, I was all yes and no at the same time, if you know what I mean.

"How about we get Mario Andretti up there to pull a U-ie and take us back to your room at the Paramount," he said. "I'll bet room service does a nice breakfast in bed," he added.

"But what about those people you thought I should meet at the poetry club?" I asked. Breakfast in bed? It occurred to me again that I didn't even know Griffin's last name. Although being a model, he might have lost it somewhere along the road.

Griffin didn't look like the happiest camper, but he nodded anyway. "Okay. You want to check it out, we can. But only because I can't resist a pretty face."

Josh would have loved it. That's what I thought when I walked into the Nuyorican Poets Café, even though I was arm in arm with Griffin. The place was way minimal. Downscale, even. Bare cement floor, dark walls, a few stage lights aimed at a mike in the front of the room, the crowd sitting around on an arrangement of orphaned tables and chairs, drinking beers and coffees. In fact, it reminded me of Drink Me, except the college grungers had been turned into Gen Xers in black. Okay, so Josh had a few black things in his wardrobe, too. He could deal.

Griffin and I took a table at the back. Griffin got us a couple of drinks and got right down to business running his hand up and down my leg. I flashed him a nervous smile and took a sip of my sparkling water. I noticed they hadn't even bothered to accessorize it with a lime.

At the mike, a skinny girl with pale skin and buzzed hennaed hair sported the red-black Vamp look on her lips and nails. So last season. I thought this place was supposed to be happening. Well, maybe Griffin knew something that I didn't. But it certainly seemed we'd come down several rungs on the hot-ticket ladder.

Meanwhile, the Vamp girl was handling the mike as if she were way friendly with it. "I think my piece is something we can all relate to," she said throatily. "I wrote it—well, actually it sort of wrote itself."

Gee, where had I heard that before?

"You know how it is when it's four A.M. and your worries are coming at you faster than you can think—"

Holy buzz cut! It was Miss Mental Existential goes New York new wave.

" 'I was alone, I am alone. City full of people, each one alone . . .' "

I looked around. The sleek black-clad crowd

was surfing on her vibes. Some of them were even practicing that same shut-eye thing those college kids had been doing at the coffeehouse that night back in California. I couldn't believe it. This was where I was going to meet someone who'd pave my road to fame and fortune? Not even.

Griffin was looking majorly intense. "She's pretty good," he said. Hel-lo! I mean, what was inside Griffin's furiously handsome head?

The audience gave her mixed reviews. A couple of rude noises but also some applause. The next guy up was better. I mean, to his credit, his classic jeans and black T-shirt wasn't the kind of look that shrieked passé. He got up and did a harmless number about his cat.

" 'Stealthily, silently, stretching sinuously . . .' " At least he didn't remind me of the dread Miss Mental Existential. The audience vote was only slightly more enthusiastic.

I leaned over and whispered to Griffin. "So, where's that editor guy you were telling me about? Is he here?"

Griffin frowned as if he'd forgotten why we'd come. "Oh." He scanned the room. "Yeah. Hey, I knew he'd make this scene. Guy over there. Black shirt, black jeans." That was everyone in the room. "Gray ponytail," he added.

"Oh, him." Not bad for an oldster. I pushed around my chair so that if the guy glanced this way, he'd have a front-row view. Griffin swiveled his seat around next to mine and put his arm around me.

"I'll introduce you when they take a break. Relax! Get into the words." He started massaging my shoulders.

I pulled away. I was buggin'. Relax? With my future at stake?

"What's the matter, Cher? Aren't you a fan of the spoken word?" he asked.

"Please. I talked my grade-point average up from a C-plus to an A-minus. I am a master of the spoken word, if I have to say so myself."

Griffin had a glint in his eye. "Yeah? You think you could do better than these other guys?"

"Who wouldn't?" I asked.

"Then go for it!" he challenged.

Oops. "But I haven't even written anything," I protested.

"Next part's open mike improv," Griffin informed me.

I felt a beat of panic. What had I gotten myself into?

"Maxwell over there will certainly notice you then," Griffin prodded, gesturing at Mr. Gray Pony-tail.

I turned that one over. Well, I supposed it was true. That was what I was here for. It couldn't hurt for that guy to see me up in front of an audience of—well, adoring fans. And I *was* pretty good at Mr. Hall's impromptu debates. How different was this? I wouldn't even have to deal with an opponent taking the opposite view. I just had to get up there and do a little patter. I looked at Maxwell. Then at Griffin, who was grinning at me as if I wouldn't dare.

Well, that did it. I can't resist a challenge. "Fine," I said. Besides, Griffin's comment about spoken words had given me an idea. "Sign me up."

And that's how I, Cher Horowitz, the only person in pale colors in a sea full of black, wound up at the mike. I was furiously scared. I told myself to pretend I was in Hall's class, but it was hard to do, seeing as there wasn't a single bandaged nose that I could spot. "I'm visiting here from California, so be nice, okay?" I told the crowd, holding the mike tight so my hands wouldn't shake.

"Yeah! Let's hear it for the Golden State," someone yelled out.

I felt encouraged. "Thank you," I said. "It is pretty golden. Especially Friday through Sunday." Quite a few people laughed. And then they stopped, which meant it was up to me to figure out what to say. It felt a little like being up front in Mr. Geist-Hall's debate class. Except that there was a zillion-watt spotlight in my face. And this was New York City. I was in Critic Central, so I knew I had to make a splash right away. I wouldn't have a chance to talk my grade up afterward. It was now or never. I contemplated doing a major about-face and heading back to——Nebraska? No way, not my style. Anyway, all they wanted me to do was talk for a little while. I mean, when was that ever a problem for me?

So with the spotlight exposing me to the world, I

calculated more or less where that Maxwell guy was sitting, flashed him my brightest Colgate and began.

"It's like this fashion thing,
It always makes my heart ring
One ring, two rings, three rings,
Whatever.

It's a fashion thing,
Of Thee I Sing
It just takes style
And a killer smile

No room for Monet
Everyone's a Bet-tay
Perfect tens
In the camera lens.

Gotta problem? It's okay,
Gone tomorrow what's here today.
Add a little here
A little less there,
Don't forget to recolor your hair.

Keep the freckle,
Lose the teeth
Make an appointment
For early next week

So like maybe this sounds kind of lame,
But I think I'll kind of stay the same
I kind of like me the way I am.
But go ahead, you can take my picture
    if you want to.

Okay, so that didn't rhyme,
It's the sentiment that's fine."

The applause was jalapeño hot. I basked in it. Maybe the Nuyorican wasn't such a random place, after all. Too bad De and Tai weren't here yelling, "Go, girl!"

I took a bow. Rising star in the limelight. Maxwell had to love me. I replaced the mike and stepped away. As my eyes readjusted to the dark room, I saw that Griffin had joined Maxwell at his table. I sent them my most righteous, sparkling smile. This was my chance!

Before joining them, I made a stopover in the ladies' room to freshen my lipstick and make sure I looked okay. At least the sign said ladies' room. There was a man and woman furiously sucking face by the sinks, and one of the "ladies" in line for the single stall looked as if she and Mother Nature might have a disagreement about what bathroom she should have been in. Great John Galliano, though. Bright red flamenco dress with a ruffled skirt, slit thigh high on one side. Excellent on a big frame. The only other person who wasn't in funeral black.

When I came out, the table where I'd last spotted Griffin was empty. It took me a moment to scope him out at the drinks counter. Maxwell Ponytail was with him. I walked up behind them, slipping on my star smile.

". . . but she just isn't right . . ." I heard Maxwell saying.

I froze. "Too wholesome, you know? Not exotic enough. You can tell she's from California. Too blond . . ."

"She could go dark," Griffin responded.

Maxwell shrugged. "She's cute, but how old is she, anyway?"

Griffin laughed. "Who knows? Anyway, I think her father's some big movie producer. Could be a big break for me."

No way. I wasn't hearing this. *His* break?

"Where's Jana, anyway?" Maxwell asked. "Or do you two have an open arrangement?"

I'd heard enough. I slunk away. I felt totally lost. I was a major bonehead. Once again, I was clueless.

A guy called to me as I went by. "Hey, great poem," he said. "New York thing. I liked that. Really."

I mustered up a weak Colgate. "Thanks," I said.

"You know, I bet you could publish that," he said.

"Really?" I stopped and gave him a more serious look. Black jeans, black T-shirt. Whatever.

"Sure," the guy said. "I have some friends who run this small press . . ."

Well, if I couldn't be a model . . .

"You'd just need to work on your vocabulary a little, maybe do something about your rhythm . . ."

I felt a spark of anger. I wasn't going to be so stupid again. Change this. Fix that. I mean, what was so awful about Cher Horowitz, high school girl from L.A.?

Griffin picked that moment to come over and

wind his arm around my waist. As if! I removed the offending object and stepped away. "Don't even think about it," I warned him. "Just hand over my phone."

"But, Cher—"

"Just hand it over." I grabbed my beige Alexander Bell and pushed through the black jeans and T-shirts to the exit.

This girl was clueless no more.

Chapter 15

*O*r was I?

So it's four A.M., and I'm so mad that it takes a few secs to realize I'm out on the streets of New York City. Me and a few challenged souls asleep on the sidewalk. And a brutally scary guy with a pin through his nose, walking a pit bull. And your basic three-piece suiter coming toward me, except he's too toasted to walk a straight line.

I gave him a wide berth. The last thing I needed right now was a slumming CEO to lose dinner on my only dress. What was I going to do now? I wandered down the street slowly. If Daddy could see me, he'd kill me. If someone else didn't beat him to it.

Josh. If I ever needed him, it was now. I was still

clutching the Alexander Bell. Should I call him for help? But what could he do three thousand miles away? Besides, he wouldn't be home, anyway. I'd figured that out by now. I had to face it. Josh was visiting the sandman with Mental Existential.

I remembered the night I'd been held up at gunpoint. Josh had driven all the way down to Sun Valley to come to my rescue. But now . . . well, to quote the Vamp, "I was alone." Nary a taxi in sight. Not that I could pay for one with the single bill I had left.

And then in the crisp, dirty predawn, I saw the most beautiful sight. Blue spikes of hair! Blue spikes held up with sugar and beer. "Wilson!" I yelled. Wilson Tyler Stratton the third was turning the corner onto my street!

He was even more shocked than I was. "Cherskie! Wassup? I can't believe it. What's a nice girl like you doing in a place like this?"

I was so majorly happy to see a friendly face that the tears just started rolling. "Hey, what's wrong?" Wilson asked.

"I'm too short and too blond, and I don't have a big enough vocabulary," I said, sniffling. "And I don't know where I am, and I don't know how to get home. . . ."

"Hey, hey, it's okay." Wilson Three wrapped me in a leather-clad hug. And that made me cry even harder. "I'll make sure you get home," he said.

The stream finally dried up, and I rubbed my eyes. I knew my makeup was trashed. But for once, I didn't care. I totally didn't. "You can get me back to the Paramount?" I asked.

"You've always had the power to get out of Oz," Wilson said. He gently eased my cellular out of my hand. He punched in a number. "Delancey Cab?" he asked. "Corner of Norfolk and Rivington," he said. "Five minutes? Dope."

"Oh, but I've only got a dollar," I said.

Wilson Three shook his spikes. "For a way phat girl like you? My treat. Well, my old man's, really," he admitted kind of sheepishly.

"Really? That's totally nice of you," I said. "Hey, what happened to the do I did?" I asked, as it suddenly hit that the spikes were back.

Wilson shrugged. "Don't take it the wrong way," he said. "I like got this look at myself in a store window and I saw my junior high school graduation picture."

I raised my eyebrows. Wilson was wrong about the do. Those spikes were a big-time don't with the shape of his face. But I just made a *W* with my fingers. "Whatever," I told him. Spikes or not, leather or shining armor, Wilson Three was my t.b. knight.

I couldn't sleep. My luxury queen-size waited for me with the cover turned down and a chocolate on my pillow. De was sacked out peacefully in the other bed. But I had too much on my mind. Besides, that little candy probably packed a whopping calorie count.

Instead, I peered into the mirror in the hotel bathroom. I sucked in my cheeks. How *would* I look minus a couple of pairs of back teeth? And suitably dark-haired. I'd have to work out a whole new color scheme for my makeup. Not to mention my wardrobe. And then I'd need to work on that extra inch or so of height. I stood on my tiptoes, my back extra straight. I pulled myself up by my hair. One little inch. How hard could that be?

I sighed noisily, and like a balloon with the air escaping, I deflated to my normal, not-quite-happening height.

"Cher?" called Dionne from the other room. Her voice was sleepily husky. "Is that you?"

"Unfortunately," I answered. "Full set of teeth and all."

"What are you talking about? What are you doing in there, anyway? What happened after we left?"

I wandered out of the bathroom and sat down cross-legged on my bed. I was nowheresville. A nobody. I felt low enough to go for the chocolate mint, gleaming at me from my pillow in its shiny green wrapper. I did it up in one bite, then reached for the one that De had resisted and placed on her nightstand.

She watched me through one half-open eye. "Uh-oh," she said as I ate the second candy. "I guess you better tell me what happened."

I nodded despondently and unloaded.

De listened like a true friend. She could have said, "I told you so." She could have reminded me that we never should have left California. But she was about as t.b. as you could possibly expect someone to be in the small hours of the morning.

"Cher," she said, "you're already in the fashion business, without being anyone but yourself."

I frowned. "I am?"

"Sure. I mean, you totally fixed up that beret woman on the airport bus, you made a shirt that was to die for out of a tablecloth. A stylist to the rich and beautiful dropped big bucks on you for those thigh-highs you spotted. And that Wilson guy's hair—you know he looked better your way."

"I guess . . ."

"I'm telling you, girlfriend . . ."

"Well. I suppose. But, De, none of that is going to get me back Josh."

De pushed herself up on one arm. "Look, you won't know what's down with him until we get back to Beverly Hills."

That didn't make me feel any better.

"Okay. Listen. I know something that'll get you psyched," De said.

I arched an eyebrow.

"We've got plastic, again," De said.

My heart soared. Suddenly everything was less bleak. "We do? What time do the stores open? What time is it now?" I bounded off my bed and pulled aside a heavy curtain. Pinky dawn was coloring the sky.

De groaned. "Cher, I'm not even awake."

"Oh, come on. It's almost light out. By the time

we have breakfast, everything will be open. We've got purchases to make, boxes to tote. We've got to get all that stuff that's on hold."

De let out a major yawn. "Cher, haven't you heard of beauty sleep? That stuff's not going to walk away on its own."

"But, De, all those too incredible clothes . . . and the presents we got for everyone back in—oh, my god. The presents. De, you have to get up right away," I said. I went over and shook her arm. "We've got to get ourselves up to the Three Roses Bakery in the Bronx. If I don't pick up those freshly baked black and whites, I might as well not bother going home at all."

Chapter 16

A ray of sunlight, a few chirping birds, and a huge traffic jam. With or without sleep it was a new day. And along with it, there was fresh plastic. What better time to use it than first thing in the morning. I could catch up on my shut-eye back in Beverly Hills. Like during third-period algebra and fourth-period French.

De and I were prepared to do it up on our last day in New York. It was time to put our credit limits to the test. And when we'd finished with the important stuff, we could take care of the minor details—like climbing the Statue of Liberty, seeing the view from the Twin Towers, visiting the Metropolitan Museum of Art, and taking a walk in Central Park. All good calorie burners, to boot.

Our first decision of the day was over transportation to the Bronx and Daddy's bakery. De wanted a red limo, and I wanted a black one.

"Black is so random, girlfriend," De said. "I mean, if you were buying it, then I could understand going for basic black, but since it's a one time only thing, why not go for it?"

I knew there was a reason that girl was my best friend. She was right, of course.

When we got picked up at the hotel, I thought for a minute that De had made a mistake and called the fire department. Our wheels were definitely red enough and big enough to be one of those hook-and-ladder things.

Once inside, however, we were sure it was a full-on limo. The way plush wall-to-wall was a bit seventies, but in a *Life Styles of the Rich and Famous* kind of time warp. All electric bar, TV, video, Muzak. A flick of a switch and De and I could have had just about anything in the world. But we opted to buzz the windows down and enjoy the sights and smells of New York City street life. Who knew when we'd be back to take in all the crime and pollution?

I was just about to zap open the bar and grab an orange juice when my cellular rang.

"I'm getting them, Daddy," I said as I clicked on. "De and I are on our way to the Three Roses."

"Three Roses?" It wasn't Daddy.

"Josh! Oh, my—" Panic city. My heart went on a roller-coaster ride. First I was all gushy that it was him. Then I remembered everything—and I got mad.

"Make him tell it like it is," Dionne said. "Don't be easy on him."

De was right. There was no reason to wait till I got back to find out where I stood. If he was a low-life two-timer, I had to know now. Also, it did seem like a red stretch limo was a way classy place to have a major argument. I knew De had to be envious.

"You know, Josh, the reason I gave you my cellular was so that you'd answer it when I called." Nice start, I thought. "So what's your lame excuse? And don't expect me to believe you, either."

"That doesn't give me much leeway, does it?" Josh said.

"Leeway?" If he didn't sound totally guilty already! As I laced into him I peeked at my Movado. Seven-thirty. That was four-thirty in the morning, California time. "So tell me, Josh, did what's-her-name send you home so she could get her beauty sleep, or did she just need to be alone at four A.M. so she could think up another complaint rock melody?"

"Miss what's-her-name?" Josh asked. I'd never heard someone play dumb so well.

"That's right, the Mental, Mental Girl. Oh, excuse me, I meant Simone."

"Simone? Oh, please, don't even start with that one again," he said. His disclaimer came accompanied with a perfect you-must-be-crazy kind of laugh.

"Well, what else am I supposed to think? Do you

have any idea how many times I tried calling you," I said.

"I'm sure I can explain, Cher," Josh said.

"So start explaining then," I said. "Like why not start with call number one. I tried you from the air, like maybe we were flying over Denver or something."

"Like maybe I was sitting in a lecture and was totally embarrassed about upstaging the professor," Josh shot back.

"And I'm sure Simone was sitting close by." Yuchh. I could hardly even say the name without wanting to hurl out the window right onto a perfectly innocent New York City sidewalk. "Well, was she?"

There was a way-too-long pause on the other end of the phone. Like either he was just plain angry, or he was thinking up some phoney excuse. "Maybe she was and maybe she wasn't," Josh finally said. "I just wasn't about to answer a telephone call in the middle of a lecture."

"Why not? I mean, you *are* in college Josh. You must know how to answer a phone by now."

Josh let out a frustrated little groan. "Just because you find it perfectly acceptable to gab long distance during school hours doesn't mean that—"

"Oh, please, save the Miss Manners bit, Josh. Haven't you been trying that one on me since I was seven? And besides, the whole reason they invented cellulars was for things like that."

Money in hand or no, I was not a happy puppy

right that second. Even in a state-of-the-art stretch, long distance fighting with Josh was an ugly thing. I hate ugly.

"Let's see, if I remember correctly, the second time the phone rang I was in the shower," Josh said.

"Whose shower?"

"I'm going to pretend I didn't hear that, Cher," Josh said, sounding so totally college. "I was head to toe shampoo and soap, but after thirty or so rings I actually thought it might be an emergency, so I tried to answer it. Did I mention that I slipped and nearly killed myself in the process?"

"But you survived," I said.

"Well, if you had let it ring twice more I would have picked up, okay?" Josh yelled back. "Now let me finish. The phone rang a third time, while I was in the library. I got about a hundred angry stares from everyone studying, so I decided I'd better answer it, quick. It was some bozo calling for Beverly Hills Pizza Boutique. Wrong number. That was my limit, Cher. After the pizza call, I decided I'd had enough of the cellular life. So I hit the no-ring button and went back to plain old living."

I wasn't sure what I should say. Was it possible that he was playing straight with me?

"Now it's your turn, Miss Sweet and Innocent," Josh said. "Would you mind telling me where you've been all night?"

Oops. The pause on my end was longer than any of his.

"It's not like *I* didn't try to call *you,* Cher. First I

tried your new basic black cellular. No answer. Then I tried your hotel room at least five times. No answer. Then I called your father to find out what was going on. He told me something about you guys getting robbed. And he also gave me some new, new cellular number. Which I also tried and got no answer."

Double oops. That must have been when Griffin had taken it away from me and stuffed it in his bag.

"So where were you, Cher?" Josh demanded. I didn't like the way he sounded so distrustful. I mean, I'd spent most of the night sweating over him.

"Okay, so I was out, big deal. It's not like we came to New York to hang out in a hotel room."

"I tried you at two-thirty your time," Josh said. "Taking a little stroll through Central Park I suppose?"

"If you really must know, I was at a big party. And then at another one. And then at a poetry slam."

"Oh. Uh-huh. Sounds like you had a lot of empty time on your hands to miss me," Josh said angrily. "And your phone—the one you never leave home without?"

"Um—well, someone took it away from me," I said, barely loudly enough for Josh to hear.

"Someone?!" The anger was shot through with hurt.

It was time to come clean. There was just no other way. And so I told him about Griffin.

"Griffin?" Josh shouted, almost puncturing my ear drum. "Who is Griffin?"

What could I say? That he was some supermodel hunk whose face is plastered on magazine covers from here to Mars? "He's just some guy who decided to drool all over me, lie to me, and do every other sleazy thing possible just to lure me into his arms."

"And *you* were jealous of *me?*" Josh asked.

"It didn't work," I assured him. "Griffin is—I mean *was* a jerk, okay? He was everything in the world that you aren't, Josh. Fake, insincere, shallow, well-dressed."

"Do you mean that, Cher?" Josh asked fondly.

I could feel this lump in my throat forming. "Of course I do," I said.

"So then why are we fighting?"

"Well, what about Simone Mental, Mental? You two didn't do any private philosophizing together while I was away? No hot-and-heavy thinking?"

Josh just laughed. "Hardly. She's a drooler, too, if you know what I mean."

I shot a thumbs-up sign to De. "So like you might be there at the airport to pick me up, big mushy kiss and all?" I asked Josh.

Josh let out a relieved laugh. "I thought that was why I called you in the first place."

Chapter 17

*A*wesome! There it is!" I exclaimed.

Dionne leaned across me to get a view out the plane window. Her face lit up in a righteous smile at the sight of—well, actually at the sight of nothing. Nothing but one thick blanket of gray smog. Which could mean only one thing—L.A. Home, sweet home.

"Air quality—poor today," I said fondly.

"Ain't it grand?" De gushed. "And may I add that next time, you're going solo."

"Hey, get honest, De," I said. "You had a pretty fab time in New York."

I mean, Griffin might have turned out to be His Sleaziness, but he *had* made it possible for us to be part of a way happening scene. Like, we'd been "this close" to Cindy's dot. How many of our friends could make the same statement?

And then, our final day touristing in our block-long red stretch hadn't been too random, either. From the Three Roses Bakery, we'd headed down to pick up Tai—who was already busy repacking the faux Samsonite. She'd be arriving back in L.A. at the end of the week.

"Whoa! I think I'll just spend the day circling the block in this baby while you guys get out and check out the sights!" Tai had said, popping the new Counting Crows album into the limo CD player and pouring herself a diet Pepsi from the minibar.

But in the end, we'd gotten her to come along on all the stops, because when you got right down to it, Tai belonged with us. That's what this trip had really been about, after all.

First stop, the Metropolitan Museum—and its awesome costume exhibit. It does seem a shame that some things aren't for sale. Then a walk in Central Park and a ride on the old-fashioned carousel. And okay, I'll admit it—I just had to have another red hot with sauerkraut and mustard before we hit the pink marble atrium of Trump Tower, collecting souvenirs in an impressive number of fancy shops.

And finally, the Twin Towers—all one-hundred and something flights to the top. No, we didn't walk. Aerobics are one thing. Stop the Insanity is another. We could see it all from up there: uptown, down-

town, Washington Square, the Lower East Side—
where I'd recited my poem—Central Park and the
round top of the carousel. We could even pick out
Tai's neighborhood across the river!

Tai admitted that she'd never bothered to take in
the view from up at the Twin Towers. "Ya know, I
wasn't even, like, sure they let you do this kind of
stuff if you weren't a tourist," she'd said.

Now, as the plane began its descent into the
glorious smog, I reminded De what a good time
we'd had. "Tell me you really would rather not have
come along," I challenged. "I mean, that new
Chanel suit you snagged at Barneys was worth the
trip alone."

De had to agree. "Yeah, okay. You're right. I
mean, I had a way fun weekend, Cher. I'll confess.
Let's just make sure we don't lose the loot at the
other end, this time."

"Not even," I assured her. Although just in case
the absolute worst happened—just in case we did a
Ground Hog Day and history managed to repeat
itself—I had the most important goods right here
with me. And I wasn't going to let go for a second.

All through the air turbulence over the Rockies,
I'd held on. All through the movie I'd mostly slept
through, all through the meal I opened but didn't
eat, I'd clutched the bakery box, tied up with string.

I held it carefully as we landed, cradling it like a
baby. The airport buildings took shape beneath us. I
felt a rush of excitement. In a few minutes, I'd be in
Josh's arms. The wheels of the plane hit the ground.

Gently. Good. I couldn't risk mangling my precious cargo.

The captain's voice came over the speakers. "Welcome to Los Angeles, ladies and gentlemen. The temperature, as always, is seventy-two degrees."

With one hand, I slapped De a limp five. With the other, I held on to my Three Roses box. Me and De and my two dozen black and whites were finally safely home where we belonged.

I was the first one off the plane and into the terminal. I spotted him immediately. Well, actually, what I spotted was the vivid, monster bouquet of tropical flowers in exotic Technicolor hues. Josh was behind there somewhere, I knew it. Yes, there were his Levi's peeking out from under the mobile garden and his arms—his strong, lean arms—holding out the flowers to me.

It was the warmest, gooiest sight in the world. I rushed toward him and threw my arms around him. Okay. I mean, I would have if I hadn't been guarding that box of black and whites and he hadn't had his arms filled with a miniature botanical garden.

But, hey, it was enough just to trade smiles and stare into each other's eyes. A private moment. No cameras, no flash bulbs, no fake Colgates. Griffin who? The guy hadn't even had a legitimate last name. Josh, on the other hand—my Josh was the real thing.

"Hey, Josh, I missed you," I told him simply.

"Cher!" Josh's voice was all hearts and cupids. He

kind of leaned around the flowers and I could almost feel his lips on—

Daddy! Hel-lo! I felt a start of surprise as I pulled back from Josh. There he was, hurrying toward our gate, looking washed out and rumpled and like he hadn't slept since I'd left for New York.

"Uh-oh," I said to Josh and De, under my breath. "Somehow, I get the feeling we're toast." Couldn't Daddy have at least waited until Josh and I had gotten in a single kiss?

I made the first move and held out the white, string-wrapped box. "Daddy!" I greeted him. "Safe and sound. I mean your cookies. All two dozen of them," I said.

Daddy just wrapped me in his arms. I could feel the box tilting over toward its side. "Wait a sec. You'll squish them," I warned him.

But Daddy held on for a way major hug. When he let go, he just shook his head. "Cher, you think I'd be late to the Warner Brothers meeting for a box of cookies? Maybe it hasn't occurred to you that I wanted to make sure my only daughter got home in one piece."

I felt another round of warm and gushy coming on. "Aw, Daddy," I said. "That's so sweet. Besides, these cookies have fifty-five grams of fat in each one, anyway."

Daddy snatched the box out of my hand. "But as long as you've brought these all the way from the Bronx . . . now, listen, I'll be home by seven sharp. And you will, too, if you know what's good for you, young lady. We have plenty to talk about. You, too," he added to Josh.

A dinner invitation. For me and my own college Baldwin. Maybe I'd been way hard on Daddy. He really had missed me. And I guess I'd missed him, too. "Wait, Daddy, let me adjust your tie," I said. But I had to kind of call it after him because he was already Audi—working the string off the box of cookies as he went.

"Now, where were we?" Josh asked. He put the huge bouquet in my arms. "Welcome home," he said, leaning in for the kiss I'd been waiting for. The scent of exotic flowers wrapped us in a little cloud of bliss. Whatever.

De cleared her throat, and we knew we'd have to save the rest of our reunion for later. But she was right about one thing: there's no place like home.

Chapter 18

*T*ai came back on Friday night. The party lasted all weekend.

Summer Kaston's parents were away at a retreat—two days of inner space, along with a private pool, meals from a top chef, and an outrageous seaside view. So Summer had generously donated their Malibu beach house for the big bash—two days of outer space, along with a private pool, meals from their live-in chef, and an outrageous seaside view.

"Umbuh-lievable," Tai pronounced, when she finally surfaced from a marathon session with Travis down on some lonely stretch of beach. "Too much. I mean you guys did this all for me?"

"No welcome home too big for our Tai," I said.

A guy who looked as if he'd been having maybe a

little too much fun made his way past us unsteadily. "Hey, great party!" he exclaimed woozily. "What's the excuse this weekend?"

I rolled my eyes. "Don't even listen to him," I told Tai. "Gotta have a few of those kind around to make the rest of us look good. The people who count know what this celebration's all about."

Tai grinned her familiar grin—one part majorly innocent, one part seen it all. "The people who count. I missed hearing stuff like that when I was in New York. Oh, hey, speaking of people who count, did I tell you my mother was taking me out for like this big welcome-home dinner—*with* Travis! Can you buh-lieve it?"

"Sure," I said, remembering how much Daddy had missed me in just one weekend. The senior generation can be so sweet sometimes.

"I guess she's gonna wait to ground me forever until after the dinner," Tai commented. "But . . . whatever."

The sun was getting ready to Audi, heading big and red toward the water. Jean-Pierre, the chef, was doing a light supper—these individual omelets filled with whatever you wanted. Christian had gotten up a rocking game of volleyball—and gotten off his shirt—the better to show off his perfect pecs. Two couples were playing chicken in the pool.

Nearby, Amber and Elton were drawing this huge crowd. I figured they were retelling—for the way hundredth time—how they'd had dinner next to— oh, who cares who. I mean, I had like tons more names to throw around after my trip, but you didn't hear me going on and on. Well, okay, at least I paused for a station break every once in a while. I was *so* annoyed with Elton and Ambular. It was great. Everything was just the way it was supposed to be.

And then there was this kind of unofficial party contest going on in various locations for the longest, most chronic kiss. Josh and I had already put in a few good tries, including a picture-perfect old-fashioned one in the swing seat on Summer's porch. Romantic, soft-focus. The right degree of yearning, but not too in-your-face. The judges, such as all we party guests were, would have to be moved. But Tai and Travis were beating us for sheer amount of time, and De and Murray had gotten in one majorly awesome kiss after an all-out screaming, yelling, fireworks, and sirens scene at the edge of the cliff overlooking the beach. Pure Hollywood, those two. De was definitely psyched to be back on the left coast.

As Tai went off to watch Travis practice his skateboard magic in the Kastons' circular driveway, Josh made his way across the lawn to me, carrying dinner for both of us. "Table with a view?" he asked. We made a little picnic on a quiet patch of grass, and watched the sun dip out of sight. The sky turned pink and orange, deepening into rose and purple. The thick air over the L.A. area holds the colors really well. And that's no lie. Pretty soon, we got into doing our thing for the kiss contest again. So, everything was back to being kind of perfect.

Well—almost. This time, Paul Devere lost about a half-dozen mini-omelets in the Kaston's antique Ming vase. Okay, so nothing and nobody's perfect. I learned that in New York. But sometimes it's pretty close.

By the way, I had to arrange to have more black and whites delivered monthly after Daddy got the bill from the hotel, the hotel minifridge, our shopping spree, the plane tickets, and the bills from three cellular phones.

But at that moment, the first star of the night appeared like a beauty mark next to the moon. The world was a righteous place. "I'm *so* glad to be back," I told Josh, the Malibu surf pounding below us. "All my natural body parts and all."

Josh laughed. "Don't ever be anyone but who you are," he said softly.

I gave him a major hug. "I totally won't."

About the Author

Jennifer Baker is the creator of Archway's Class Secrets series. She is also the author of two dozen young adult and middle-grade novels, including the First Comes Love series and books in the Sweet Valley High series. Jennifer Baker lives in New York City with her husband and son.